THE FIDDLER'S SECRET

The Riverboat Adventures

1. *Escape Into the Night*
2. *Race for Freedom*
3. *Midnight Rescue*
4. *The Swindler's Treasure*
5. *Mysterious Signal*
6. *The Fiddler's Secret*

Adventures of the Northwoods

1. *The Disappearing Stranger*
2. *The Hidden Message*
3. *The Creeping Shadows*
4. *The Vanishing Footprints*
5. *Trouble at Wild River*
6. *The Mysterious Hideaway*
7. *Grandpa's Stolen Treasure*
8. *The Runaway Clown*
9. *Mystery of the Missing Map*
10. *Disaster on Windy Hill*

THE RIVERBOAT ADVENTURES

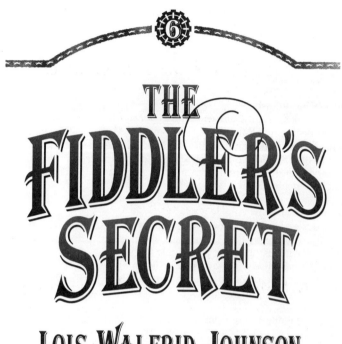

THE FIDDLER'S SECRET

LOIS WALFRID JOHNSON

BETHANY HOUSE PUBLISHERS
MINNEAPOLIS, MINNESOTA 55438

Cover illustration by Angelo
Cover design by the Lookout Design Group
Story illustrations by Paul Casale
Side-wheeler illustration by Toni Auble
Map of Upper Mississippi by Meridan Mapping
Sign language chart courtesy of the Illinois School for the Deaf, Jacksonville.

Scripture quotations are from the King James Version of the Bible.

Published by Bethany House Publishers
A Ministry of Bethany Fellowship International
11370 Hampshire Avenue South
Minneapolis, Minnesota 55438
www.bethanyhouse.com

Printed in the United States of America by
Bethany Press International, Minneapolis, Minnesota 55438

Library of Congress Cataloging-in-Publication Data

CIP data applied for

ISBN 1–55661–356–3   CIP

To

Justin Kevin,
Karin Lyn,
Jennifer Christine,
and
Elise Grace

because I love you!

LOIS WALFRID JOHNSON is the bestselling author of more than twenty-five books. Her work has been translated into twelve languages and has received many awards, including the Gold Medallion, the C. S. Lewis Silver Medal, the Wisconsin State Historical Society Award, and five Silver Angels from Excellence in Media. Yet Lois believes that one of her greatest rewards is knowing that readers enjoy her books.

In her fun times Lois likes to camp, bike, cross-country ski, be with family and friends, and talk with young people like you. Lois and her husband, Roy, live in Minnesota.

In the time in which this book is set, African-Americans were called *Negro*, the Spanish word for black, or *colored people*.

Native Americans were called *Indians*.

Contents

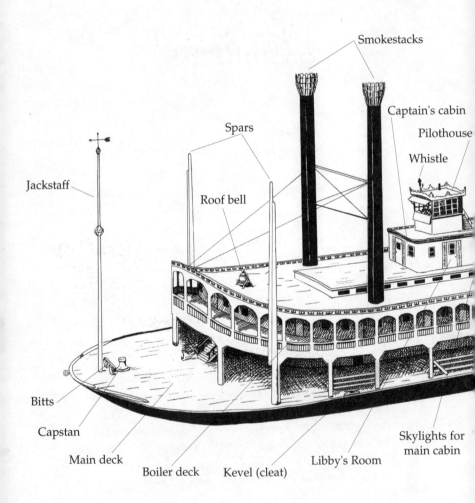

Smokestacks

Captain's cabin

Pilothouse

Whistle

Spars

Roof bell

Jackstaff

Bitts

Capstan

Main deck

Boiler deck

Kevel (cleat)

Libby's Room

Skylights for
main cabin

The Side-Wheeler Christina

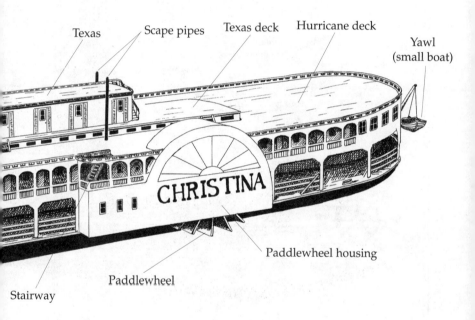

Texas

Scape pipes

Texas deck

Hurricane deck

Yawl
(small boat)

CHRISTINA

Paddlewheel housing

Paddlewheel

Stairway

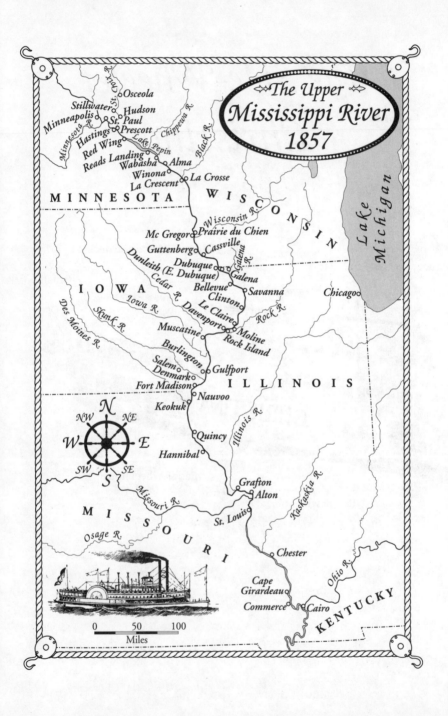

1

Night of Fear

*I*n the dark of night, Libby Norstad suddenly woke up. *Where am I?* She wondered as she struggled to think. *What woke me?*

A dream? A nightmare? Whatever the cause, Libby shivered with fear.

Soon after midnight her father's steamboat had left Galena, Illinois, heading up the Mississippi River. But now Libby felt no movement, heard no engines or slap of paddle wheels against the water.

It's quiet. Too quiet. Even the night air felt heavy and strange.

Then from near at hand the ship's bell broke the silence. As rapid strokes rang out, then stopped, Libby knew it was a signal.

What's wrong? she wondered. *What happened? Where's Pa?*

With a trembling heart, she leaped up and changed into her dress. As she stepped onto the deck outside her room, the cold fingers of fog seemed to clutch her.

Libby gasped. Without thinking she stretched out her hands to feel the way. As she peered into the darkness, she could not see even eight feet ahead.

"Pa!" she cried in terror. "Where are you?"

Her hand against the outer wall of her room, Libby crept forward. When she reached her father's cabin at the front of the *Christina*, it was empty. Feeling as if she were sleepwalking, Libby turned around and started back.

Silly! she told herself, ashamed of her fear. *I'm on my father's boat. Why am I afraid?*

But the bell rang again, cutting through the ragged edges of her nerves. Forcing herself to be calm, she headed for the stairway.

In the four years after her mother's death, Libby had stayed with her aunt in a mansion along Chicago's Gold Coast. For the past five months, Libby had been with her father. In that August of 1857, she was still learning to face the dangers of living on a steamboat.

I want to be strong, she thought. *But I just feel scared!*

When Libby reached the deck below, it was even darker. Usually filled with first-class passengers, the boiler deck was just above the large boilers that heated water and created steam to run the engines. With not one person in sight, the deck was strangely quiet. Libby had only one thought—to find Pa, her friend Caleb Whitney, or someone who would help her feel safe.

Instead, Libby found the railing and followed it toward the front of the boat. Through the murky darkness she saw someone standing at the bow. Libby's heart leaped with relief. *Annika Berg!*

The young woman's long black hair was pulled up to fall in loose curls at the back of her head. During the past week the teacher had helped Libby and her friends in a time of danger. Working with the Underground Railroad, the secret plan that helped slaves escape to freedom, Annika had given them a place to stay. In a few short days, Libby had grown to love her.

As Libby took another step, Annika heard her and turned. "Come enjoy the view with me!"

Libby giggled. "What a view! Solid fog!" For the first time since waking up, she felt better.

Annika stood at the railing, peering down. "I've been trying to see if the ropes are out. We must be tied up along the riverbank. Right?"

Libby nodded. She could barely see the line, or rope, between the boat and the small willows along the river's west bank.

Annika faced her. "We're here because the pilot can't see, your father can't see—"

"Yes." Not wanting to talk about her fears, Libby tried to cut Annika off. But Libby's thoughts leaped on. *We're here so we don't run into a sandbar. So the sharp roots of a tree caught in the river bottom don't pierce our hull. So we don't run into another boat. Or another—*

"Are we far enough out of the channel?" Annika echoed Libby's thoughts. "Could a boat crash into us?"

Libby's hands knotted. It was her biggest fear. *If I don't admit it, maybe it won't happen.*

Now she wished it were Caleb talking to Annika. Though Libby was thirteen and Caleb only one year older, he always seemed to answer questions better. A conductor for the Underground Railroad since the age of nine, Caleb had years of practice in being questioned by people not as nice as Annika.

The teacher met Libby's gaze. "If a captain thinks he needs to keep going—"

The ship's bell broke into her words. Then Libby remembered. On a steamboat tied up in fog, its crew rang the bell rapidly for five seconds out of every minute.

When the bell was quiet, Annika waited for Libby's answer. "The lines hold us as close to the shore as we can be without hurting the paddle wheel on this side," she said. "We can't get any farther out of the channel. We're long and wide, and the stern drifts out with the current."

"And a boat that doesn't wait for the fog to lift can run into us?" Annika's blue eyes were dark with concern. "Why doesn't your father just tell people to go on shore?"

In that moment Libby felt impatient with Annika's questions. Then Libby remembered that Annika was used to taking care of people—children in her classroom, fugitive slaves. Annika was used to thinking ahead.

Just the same, Libby felt she had to defend her father. Because of her, Annika and Pa had gotten off to a bad start. *I want Annika to think the best of him. To see Pa as a hero.*

"If we stay on the boat, there's a danger that something might happen," Libby said. "But we hope it won't. If we go on shore in the dark, it's pretty sure we won't like what we find."

"Such as?"

Libby shrugged. "I can't see what's here. I just know we're between towns, and there are islands in the river. If a riverboat captain finds a criminal on board and it's a long way to the next stop, the captain puts the man off on an island."

"Because it's a serious crime, and the captain has no choice?" Annika asked.

"If he knows his passengers might be harmed," Libby said.

Annika's voice was filled with respect. "I had no idea a riverboat captain has to deal with all that."

Libby smiled. *Now I'm getting somewhere*, she thought smugly. *I'll make sure Annika likes Pa. But I'll be clever this time.* From past experience Libby knew she had to be careful. Annika had already made it clear that she didn't want anyone to think she was looking for a husband.

"I don't know what else we'd find," Libby went on. "Some places there would be sink-down-deep mud, reeds, and tall grasses. Maybe floating bogs. Snakes."

"Snakes?"

"Copperheads. Timber rattlesnakes. This time of year, they live along the river bottoms."

"I see."

"Even in the fog." To Libby's surprise she already felt better. Annika could understand how Libby dreaded snakes and criminals and fog. *It would be nice having her around all the time.*

Now Libby knew just what to say. "Pa is a courageous man. A riverboat captain has to be very brave. . . ."

Her eyes wide, Annika listened.

"And wise and good." Libby spoke quickly to make sure she got it all in. "He cares about his passengers. That's what makes him a good family man, a good choice for anyone who marries him."

Annika backed off. "Well," she said, "as long as I know we're in good hands, I'll leave you now."

Inwardly Libby groaned. *I did it again.* Libby wished she could bite off her tongue.

Instead she exclaimed, "No, don't go!" Already the fog seemed to close around her. Having Annika there pushed aside

Libby's fear. "I'll show you the lantern that tells other boats we're here."

Together they walked along the deck closest to the river channel. As they drew near the stern, the light of the lantern welcomed them. Yet the fog seemed even thicker than before.

"I wonder how far a pilot can see the light," Annika said.

Before she could answer, Libby heard the long, deep blast of a steamboat whistle. A whistle saying, "I'm coming! Get out of my way!"

Like a nightmare it was—a nightmare so real that Libby trembled. As the *Christina's* bell rang without stopping, Libby shouted into the fog, "Watch out! We're here!"

But the deep whistle sounded again, closer now. Then Libby heard the slap of paddle wheels against water. With Annika at the rail beside her, Libby peered into the night.

Moments later a deckhand on the other boat called to his pilot. The front of the steamboat loomed up out of the fog. Frantically, Libby waved her arms. "We're here! Watch out! We're here!"

Now Libby saw the railing along an upper deck, the men standing as lookouts. As a deckhand called another warning, Libby's heart leaped with fear. "Don't run into us!"

But the steamboat whistle cut through her words, and Libby knew. *No one can hear a word I'm saying!*

Filled with panic, she grabbed Annika's arm and yanked her away from the railing. "Run!"

With Annika close behind, Libby raced to the other side of the boat. When Libby dropped down on her stomach, Annika fell to the deck beside her.

Hands over her head, face against the boards, Libby braced herself for the crash.

In that instant of waiting, she had one thought. *I don't want anything to happen to Annika!*

2

Secret Face

*S*econds later, Libby felt a jolt run through the boat. Timbers snapped. Flying pieces landed with a thud. Frightened voices cried out. From the pens near the stern, cows bawled and sheep bleated.

In the wake of the other boat, the *Christina* rocked up and down. Riding wave after wave, she swung out against her lines. Then the slap of paddles and sound of engines moved farther and farther away.

On the boiler deck where Libby lay, first-class passengers spilled out of their rooms. From the main deck below, people called out in different languages. Still frozen by fright, Libby felt she could not move.

After what seemed like hours, she lifted her head. "Annika?"

The teacher lay with her head covered and face down.

"Annika?" Libby pushed herself up to a sitting position. "Are you okay?"

Annika sat up. "I'm fine, Libby." Reaching out, she squeezed Libby's hand. "It was a close call, wasn't it?"

"I'm glad you ran." Libby's teeth chattered, and her body trembled. She was still shaking with fright when Caleb Whitney reached them.

"Libby!" Caleb knelt down on the deck beside her. "Are you hurt?"

Even in the fog and darkness, Libby could see Caleb's blond hair and the worry in his blue eyes. Five years ago Pa had asked Caleb's grandmother to be head pastry cook. Caleb had lived on board ever since.

"Were you here when the boat passed?" he asked.

Libby nodded, still too shaken to speak. Drawing a deep breath, she tried to hide how scared she felt. "One minute before, Annika and I stood at the railing, close to the stern. That's where it hit, isn't it?"

Caleb nodded. "How did you get here?"

Libby forced herself to smile. "We ran."

"Are you all right, Annika?" Caleb asked as he helped her up.

"Thanks to Libby." Annika pushed back the hair that had fallen over her eyes.

Libby was angry now. "How could any steamboat captain keep running with the fog the way it is?"

"He must have a very good reason." Caleb studied her face. "You really are scared, aren't you?"

Libby swallowed hard. "The deckers—the passengers on the main deck. Even if the boat didn't hit them directly—" Libby stopped, afraid to put her thoughts into words.

"I know." Caleb's voice was too quiet. "I was there when the boat hit. There's more than a hundred people on that deck. The jolt could have knocked a lot of them into the water. As far as I can tell, no one fell in."

As Caleb gave Libby a hand up, her gaze met his. "You're just as scared as I am."

"Not quite." Caleb's face held no fear, but Libby knew her friend well. When Caleb helped runaway slaves, he couldn't take the risk of one wrong expression. For a fugitive it might mean the difference between life and death. Caleb had learned to hide his feelings.

"Pa?" Libby asked, still shivering.

"I haven't seen him yet." Pulling off his jacket, Caleb gave it to Libby.

She was glad for its warmth. "It was so hot today, it's hard to believe it's cold now."

"That's what brings fog," Caleb reminded her. "The river is still warm. If a wind comes up or the sun burns off the fog, your pa will go on."

In spite of Caleb's jacket, Libby shivered again. Then she felt glad. "Pa runs a good ship, doesn't he?"

Caleb's grin was real now. "The best. I don't want anything to hurt him."

His words were so similar to what Libby had thought about Annika that it gave her a strange feeling. Having something happen to his passengers would hurt Pa very much. Whoever they were, whether rich or poor, slave or free, he cared about them.

As the *Christina*'s bell rang again, the high notes of a fiddle pierced the fog and darkness. The happy sound set Libby's feet moving. "Let's go see who's playing. Maybe we'll find Jordan and Peter."

On their way to find the fiddler, they returned to the stern to see what had happened. On the channel side of the boat, a long piece of railing was splintered. At the place where Libby and Annika had stood, the railing was torn away, leaving a large hole in the deck.

Annika took one look and quietly said, "Thank you, Libby." Gazing up at the nighttime sky, she spoke again. "Thank you, Lord."

A moment later Pa found them. In his captain's uniform he looked tall and handsome. Yet for Libby Pa always meant more—the kind of father he was. For as long as she could remember, Libby had been proud of him.

Seeing her there, Pa looked relieved. *He's checking on me*, Libby thought, feeling warm inside. *He cares about me.*

Then Pa's gaze passed on to Annika. "Good to see you, Miss Berg. You're all right?"

Annika smiled. "I'm fine, Captain Norstad."

Libby felt pleased that Pa was concerned about Annika too. After their bad start, maybe they would be good friends.

"Thanks to Libby, I'm fine," Annika added. When she told the story, Pa's face turned white.

"And this is where you stood?" Pa motioned to the hole in the deck. "Come here, Libby. Let me give you a big hug." As Pa's arms went around her, Libby felt safe again.

A moment later the ship's carpenter and his crew joined them. "We have a lot to be grateful for," Pa told them. "No one was hurt, and the damage could have been much worse. Block it off here so no one falls over. Then go down and work on the main deck."

Leaving Pa behind, Libby, Caleb, and Annika took the stairs in the middle of the *Christina* to see the rest of the damage. On the main deck, the passing boat had ripped open the animal pens. At least twenty feet of the guard, the part of the boat that extended out over the hull, was torn away.

Near the stern an owner hung on to a rope around his cow's neck. Another man worked to keep his sheep away from the edge. Libby knew it was a miracle that no one had been hurt.

The fiddler was still playing, and Libby, Caleb, and Annika followed the sound of his music. At the front of the boat they found Peter sitting at the top of the wide stairway overlooking the bow. Libby's Newfoundland, a great black dog named Samson, lay beside him.

Jordan Parker sat two steps below. A runaway slave, he had found safety on the *Christina* and stayed on to work for Pa. When Caleb sat down next to Jordan, Libby and Annika squeezed in beside Peter.

To Libby, Peter Christopherson seemed like the younger brother she had always wanted. An orphan who lost his hearing through illness, Peter had lived on the *Christina* for about a month. Now Libby felt so glad to see him that she gave him a quick hug. Peter looked surprised, then grinned.

"Are you okay?" Libby asked, using signs.

"I'm okay," the blond ten-year-old answered in the way he had of always taking care of himself. Peter had learned sign language at the school for the deaf in Jacksonville, Illinois. Now Libby and the others were learning sign language from him.

Though unable to hear, Peter spoke well. "You too?" he asked.

Libby nodded, but inside she didn't feel so sure. Whenever her mind jumped back to those moments just before the other boat hit the *Christina*, she trembled. The sound of pounding hammers reminded Libby of her close escape.

On the main deck, a lantern hung just beyond the bottom of the stairs. Its soft light pierced the before-dawn darkness and fog. The fiddler stood nearby, his bow dancing over the strings.

Around him the deck passengers sat on crates and barrels or stood wherever there was room. Crammed into whatever space they could find, the deckers tapped their toes in time to the music.

Annika tipped her head toward the fiddler and whispered, "He's really good."

Young and slender, the fiddler had dark hair that nearly reached his shoulders, a mustache, straight nose, and high cheekbones. He stood near an immigrant's trunk, but Libby wondered about it. *Is it his? Something doesn't quite fit.*

Even from where she sat, Libby could see that the fiddler's white shirt looked tattered. It seemed strange. Deck passengers were usually short of money, but the immigrants among them worked hard and kept their clothes mended.

Maybe the fiddler doesn't know how to mend his clothes, Libby thought. *Maybe he's traveling alone.*

Libby's mind leaped to Pa. *Traveling alone. It's been over four years since Ma died. All that time Pa's been alone.*

From her place at one side of the steps, Libby looked up to see her father. As Pa started down, he smiled again at Libby and Annika. For a moment Pa stopped to talk with Peter and Jordan, then continued down the steps.

While the fiddler played on, Pa moved from one group of people to the next. Often he stopped to talk with an immigrant family. More than once Pa pointed to a child, then to the edge of the deck. Each time Pa motioned as though to keep the child away, a father or mother nodded. Though Pa didn't speak their language, they seemed to understand.

At last Pa returned to the bottom of the stairs. Standing near the wall where the lantern hung, he watched and listened.

The fiddler's bow moved faster and faster, attacking the strings with short, quick movements. In the fog and darkness, his melodies reached out to the people who listened. Catching the rhythm of the music, they clapped along with him.

Then, as the fiddler played, he began to dance. Wherever they could, passengers pushed back more freight. In the small open space the fiddler stomped his feet, whirling about.

When a little girl stood up, people crowded back still farther, making room. Her bare feet flying across the boards, the girl twirled and turned. An even smaller boy climbed onto a crate and jumped up and down with the music.

As the fiddler stepped back out of the circle, his music swept on, light and free. Other dancers filled the space.

Clapping with the deckers, Caleb and Jordan stomped their feet and called out for more songs. Peter watched the boys to catch the rhythm, then joined in the clapping.

Sometimes the fiddler plucked the strings. Other times he bowed two strings at once. From one happy song to the next he went, his music driving back the fog and darkness.

Looking around, Libby knew the night had changed. Already the deckers had left their terror behind. Though the fog still closed them in, the deck rocked with music and laughter.

Only once did Libby see the fiddler's gray-blue eyes. *He knows*, she thought. *He knows the music sends away their fear.*

Yet strangely, Libby felt uneasy about the man. *His face holds a secret. Who is he? Why is he here?*

Puzzled by her uneasiness, Libby kept watching the fiddler. *Why do I think he has a secret?*

Then she noticed something else. Though his tattered clothes made him seem poor, he hadn't put out a hat to collect money.

For some time Pa waited, as though not wanting to rob the deckers of their fun. When the fiddler stopped playing, the crowd cheered and clapped. Only then did Pa step forward.

"Please," Pa invited. "Will you play for my first-class passengers?"

When the man looked as if he didn't understand, Pa pointed to the fiddler and his fiddle. Then Pa pointed up the wide stairs to the large main cabin that served as dining room.

The fiddler shook his head. *"Nein!"* It sounded as if he were saying *nine*, but Libby knew it was the German word for *no*.

"I would be greatly pleased if you would do this for me," Pa answered. "My passengers love fine music and would be honored to have you play."

The fiddler shook his head. "It is not *gut!*"

Hearing the word *good*, Libby listened to the man's accent. Though he used German words, Libby wondered if he came from Germany. For some reason the fiddler didn't sound quite like her German friend, Elsa.

"Come." Pa drew the fiddler away from the passengers who were listening. "I'm not asking you to play for nothing. I'll pay you for your concert."

For an instant the fiddler wavered, as though trying to make up his mind. *There's fear in his eyes,* Libby thought. *I wonder why.*

3

Big Bullies

$\mathcal{T}$he fiddler motioned to his tattered shirt. "My clothes?"

"If they bother you, you can wear some of mine," Pa answered. "We're about the same size."

"Nein!" the fiddler exclaimed, even more strongly than at first.

Backing off, Pa smiled. "Wear whatever you like. You look fine the way you are."

Strange! Libby thought. *I've never seen Pa do that.* His first-class passengers were well clothed, well traveled, and well educated. The people Pa hired to entertain them were always dressed well unless playing a part. But Libby knew her father. He would not want to embarrass the fiddler.

"You will be my special guest," Pa said.

This time the fiddler nodded. "I will come."

"Tonight? After our evening meal?"

The fiddler smiled. "I will play a concert your passengers will remember forever."

Pa turned to where Caleb and Jordan still sat on the steps. "Spread the word. Tell the first-class passengers we'll have the best concert they've ever heard."

The fog had changed to a milky white when Libby sat down to breakfast in the large main cabin that was the dining room. As though Caleb's grandmother also wanted to help people forget the accident, she had outdone herself on the food. When Libby caught a glimpse of Gran in the doorway, her cheeks were flushed with the heat of the oven. But Gran's cinnamon rolls and one-of-a-kind breakfast had never been better.

After breakfast Libby found Caleb and Jordan on the main deck. Sitting down on a crate next to them, she said, "I wonder why the fiddler is going to Minnesota Territory."

Jordan grinned. "Probably for the same reason I'm going. To see what's there."

Libby felt curious. Both she and Caleb had expected Jordan to stay in Galena, Illinois. After years of separation because of slavery, everyone in his family was there. "Why *are* you going to St. Paul?"

Jordan dropped his voice to a mysterious whisper. "To spy out the land."

"Like the spies in the Bible who went to the Promised Land?" At his birth Jordan's mother had named him in the belief he would lead his people out of slavery across the river to the Promised Land of freedom. For many slaves that meant the Ohio River. For others, such as Jordan's family, it meant crossing the Mississippi River and the state of Illinois to reach Canada.

"Do you mean your family would move to St. Paul?" Libby asked.

"Depends on what I find. My momma and daddy like livin' in Galena, but it's fearful close to where we were slaves."

"But Minnesota Territory? Pa said that slave owners go to St. Paul and Stillwater to escape the heat in summer."

"Aw, Libby, don't you get all worried now."

"I mean it. People from the South like the cooler weather."

Jordan grinned. "It's been five months since I ran away from Riggs. He's got so many slaves he's forgotten me."

"Five months since he told you a slave never got away from him alive," Libby answered. "Right this minute there could be men like him on the *Christina*. Men who know about the reward on your head. They could be coming north to take their families home. Couldn't they, Caleb?"

"Maybe. Maybe not." Caleb pushed his blond hair out of his eyes. "There's one thing sure. On the trip back down the river, Jordan will have to be extra careful."

Libby still felt uneasy. "It's only August seventeenth. Lots of time for hot weather still." But Jordan only shrugged his shoulders.

He's brave, I know, Libby thought as she left the boys and went up to the hurricane deck. More than once she had admired Jordan's bravery. *But sometimes he has so much courage that he runs straight into trouble!*

As the morning sun burned off the fog, the *Christina* headed upriver again. When the side-wheeler tied up at a small town, Libby looked down from her favorite viewing spot to see what was going on.

Roustabouts, or rousters, had begun unloading freight. On the riverfront nearby, three boys were teasing a small dog. When he leaped out of the arms of the youngest boy, the dog dodged this way and that, trying to get away.

Soon the biggest boy cornered the dog next to a pile of freight. Picking him up, the bully held the dog so tightly that he squealed with fear. Squirming and twisting, he struggled to get away.

Angry at the cruelty she saw, Libby headed for the steps. When she reached the main deck, she found Peter ahead of her.

As he hurried down the gangplank, he called to the boys. "Stop it!"

The biggest boy whirled around. Still holding the dog, the boy stalked over. More than a head taller, the bully glared down at Peter. "Who do you think you are?"

"Stop hurting that dog!" Peter answered without giving away that he hadn't heard one word.

Instead, the boy walked over to the river. There he dunked the dog in the water, then rolled him in the brown, sandy mud of the riverbank. Still squirming, the dog yelped with fear. The more he struggled, the tighter the bully held him.

"Stop it!" Peter exclaimed. Rushing forward, he tried to take the dog from the bully. Instead, the older boy stepped back. The two other boys moved behind Peter, surrounding him.

By the time Libby reached them, she was so angry that she

had lost all fear. "Put that dog down," she commanded.

"A girl now!" the biggest bully sneered at Peter. "So a girl has to rescue you!"

The bully pointed at Libby. Peter caught his meaning and flushed. "I can handle this," he told her.

Libby refused to leave. She glared at the biggest bully. "Let go of that dog, or else!"

The boy laughed. "Or else what?"

As though expecting the dog to bite Libby, the bully set him down in front of her. Instead, the dog danced out of arm's length, planted his spindly legs, and barked at the bully. *Yap, yap, yap!*

But his freedom didn't last. Though the dog darted away, the youngest bully caught him.

Upset by the dog's squeals, Libby balled her fists. The minute the youngest bully looked up, she struck him in the nose. As blood gushed out of his nostrils, the boy dropped the dog.

Horrified, Libby stepped back. But Peter rushed forward, grabbed the dog, and headed for the gangplank. "Run for it!" he cried.

Her knees weak, Libby felt she couldn't move. Then the tallest bully whirled around and started toward her. Libby leaped away and kept running. By the time she raced up the gangplank, she was out of breath.

From the safety of the main deck, she looked back. Already the other bullies were teasing the boy with the bloody nose. Peter found Caleb and Jordan.

Caleb looked from Peter to Libby. "Hey! What's up?"

Peter grinned. "Libby gave a boy a bloody nose!"

"Really?" Caleb asked Libby. "The society girl from Chicago gave a boy a bloody nose?"

Libby was embarrassed. "Peter, be quiet!" Then she remembered their sign for "Shush!"

But Peter kept on. "She hauled off and hit him! You better watch out, Caleb. Don't *ever* make Libby mad!"

Caleb grinned at her. "I can't do that. Not make her mad, I mean. But from now on I'll watch out."

"What did you say?" Peter asked.

Palms up, Caleb waved his hands to tell him, "Not important." Instead, Caleb pointed to the dog. The mud was drying, drawing the dog's hair into clumps.

Peter wore a pleased-with-himself grin. "I'm going to help people," he announced.

Libby took Peter's slate from the bag over his shoulder. "Help people?" she wrote. "Dogs aren't people!"

Peter looked disgusted. "This dog is going to help your pa."

That was an even bigger puzzle for Libby. "How?"

"Your pa needs a watchdog."

"What about Samson?" Libby wrote.

"Samson is a happy dog," Peter said quickly as though to keep peace. "He'll push you away if there's danger. He'll jump in to rescue people from the water. But this dog—my dog—will make noise. All the way up the gangplank I could feel him barking."

Libby grinned. "He made noise, all right." Holding her hands in front of her chest, Libby curled her fingers as if they were paws. "Yap, yap! Yap, yap, yap!"

Peter seemed to read her lips. He understood the barking.

"So," Libby wrote, "this dog is supposed to help Pa?"

Peter nodded. "I'll train him to do that. Of course, he'll have to help me too."

"Of course." Libby glanced toward Caleb, who had swallowed his laughter. "What color is your dog?"

When Peter didn't answer, Caleb took the slate from Libby. "You can't just pick up a dog and start to own it. It might belong to someone."

"He doesn't," Peter said. "This dog is an orphan." His arms closed around the dirty creature. "I know."

Yes, you would, Libby thought, suddenly filled with compassion. After being an orphan himself, Peter would recognize it in a dog.

Caleb wasn't going to let Peter off so easily. "We need to check with the men who live here. Jordan and I will go with you. Those bullies won't touch you if we're around."

With the dog in his arms, Peter started down the gangplank. The minute his feet touched the riverbank, the three boys started toward him. When Peter saw them, he stopped and stood his ground.

The biggest bully walked straight up to him and held a fist in front of Peter's face. "So! The little boy is back!"

As if he had heard the bully's words, Peter glared at him without speaking.

The bully motioned to his friends. "C'mon, let's get the mutt!"

The other boys moved close. The biggest bully leaned over Peter, scowling down at him.

Just then Caleb and Jordan walked up. Standing behind Peter, Caleb and Jordan glared at the three bullies. Now that they were evenly matched, the bullies weren't so eager to take on a fight. One by one, they walked away.

A short time later, Peter returned to the boat. The front of his shirt was filthy from hugging the mutt, but his eyes glowed with the news he had for Libby. "Caleb asked questions for me. My dog is an orphan, all right. The men who work on the wharf say he's hung around for three weeks. He lives on crusts of bread people throw him."

When Peter let the dog down, he ran to a deck passenger. Sitting on his haunches, the dog eyed the man's food, wiggled his tail, and barked.

Peter hurried over and scooped up the dog. "He's thin now, but I'll find the right food for him. Caleb's grandmother will help me."

"What's your dog's name?" Libby signed.

Peter's eyes filled with pride. "His name is Wellington."

"Why do you call him that?" Libby wrote.

"It's the right name for such a good dog. The Duke of Wellington defeated Napoleon at the Battle of Waterloo."

Often Libby felt surprised by the bits of information Peter knew. Now he went on. "This dog puts up a good fight. You'll see. He's been fighting for life."

"He's been fightin' for his life, all right," Jordan said. "I can recognize the signs."

Libby had no doubt about that either. The next time Peter let the dog down, Libby backed away so he couldn't touch her. Even from a distance he smelled.

When Wellington scampered off, Peter chased after him, and Libby felt relieved. "He's naming that dirty little mutt after the Duke of Wellington?"

Caleb glared at her. "This is serious business for Peter. Don't make fun of him."

As Libby met Caleb's eyes, she knew she had better not say another word. Though she didn't want the dog mistreated, she wasn't sure she could handle another dog on board. Getting used to Samson had been hard enough.

When Peter found a large tub and a bucket, Jordan helped him draw water from the river. As soon as the tub was full, Peter lifted the dog into the water. Wellington fought against him, but Peter hung on. Sloshing water over the dog's back and head, he rubbed him down with soap. Though Wellington yipped and whimpered, Peter kept washing him.

Soon Peter lifted the dog from the water. Wellington was so thin that Libby caught her breath. With his wet hair plastered against his body, she could see every rib. His legs seemed to be only skin and bone.

How long has it been since the dog had a good meal? Libby wondered.

Caleb emptied the dirty water into the river, and Jordan filled the tub again. As Jordan went back and forth carrying water, Libby noticed a man watching him. Still thinking about the possibility of a slave catcher, Libby felt concerned. Then she realized the man was the fiddler.

Once again Peter soaped Wellington down. By the time the water turned gray, Wellington had changed color.

"He's brown!" Libby exclaimed, then remembered to point to the dog's coat so Peter would understand.

The ten-year-old grinned. "I told you he's a good dog."

"Being brown doesn't make a dog good," Libby spouted, then remembered to use signs.

Smudges of mud covered Peter's face and shirt. More smudges darkened his wet sleeves.

With the third tub of water, Wellington changed colors again. To Libby's amazement his coat looked brownish red.

By now Wellington had begun responding to Peter's love. Lifting the dog out of the final rinse water, Peter wrapped a towel around him and set him on the deck. As Peter rubbed the dog dry, Wellington crept closer to him.

Suddenly Caleb started to laugh. "Libby, the color of Wellington's hair is exactly the same as yours!"

4

Shadowman!

*L*ibby scowled at Caleb. She couldn't think of anything she wanted less than hair the color of a dog's. Especially a dog such as Wellington!

But Caleb was already pointing to Wellington's hair, then to Libby's. When both Peter and Jordan caught on, they, too, started laughing. Libby's face burned with embarrassment.

"How can you, Caleb Whitney!" Libby's auburn hair had always been a source of pride to her. Here on the deck, the sunlight brought out the deep red and gold. It also reminded Libby of the sacrifice she had made for Peter in cutting her long hair.

In that moment he stopped laughing, as if he, too, remembered. "Libby, your hair looks really nice."

Surprised by his kindness, Libby blinked her eyes. When she stopped being angry, she saw that Wellington had a long, narrow head and a wiry coat. Even Libby had to admit that it was a wiry *red* coat.

"I think he's some kind of terrier," Caleb wrote on the slate.

"He's a *mutt*!" Libby spit out.

"My family used to have a dog like him," said Peter, blissfully unaware of Libby's opinion. "He always perked up his ears when I came home. Then he jumped up to welcome me."

Though Wellington was still wet, Peter gathered him close. Wellington snuggled his nose into the crook of Peter's arm.

Seeing them together, Libby felt just a bit kinder. *Maybe he won't be such a bad dog after all. Except for his size, Wellington isn't that much different from Samson. And somehow I grew to love him.* Reaching out, Libby even petted the terrier's wet head.

As Libby got ready for the concert that evening, she brushed her hair and felt thankful that Annika had trimmed it. Libby still missed the long, beautiful hair she had cut, but at least it looked even now. In the damp night air it even curled in a special way.

By the time she left her room, the sun had set. When Libby started down the stairs, wisps of fog hung just above the surface of the river. As she watched, fingers of fog reached upward. Soon the small wisps gathered together, changing shape. Twisting and turning, they rose in the air.

Uneasy now, Libby dreaded the thick fog they might once again face. Like a column of smoke, it hung in the darkness.

Soon she entered the main cabin, the long, beautiful room

that stretched from one end of the boat to the other. The tables used during meals had been pushed against the walls, and chairs were set row by row for a concert. Overhead, oil lamps glowed softly, pushing away Libby's thoughts of fog and danger.

Wearing white jackets, Caleb and Jordan stood along the back wall. Though they were cabin boys for Pa, both of them did much more. While Libby talked with them, the fiddler came in.

"I think he has a secret," Libby whispered as the man walked toward the other end of the room. "Maybe he's a long-lost son, hiding from his family."

"Or maybe he made his family angry." Caleb's grin was full of teasing for Libby.

Jordan laughed. "You both have too much imagination. I think he's a son lookin' for his family."

The fiddler held his violin under his arm and still wore the tattered white shirt. It bothered Libby. In spite of her uneasiness about him, she liked the way he helped the deckers after the crash. Libby didn't want first-class passengers making fun of him.

At the front of the room the fiddler sat down. A murmur passed through the crowd. It wasn't hard for Libby to guess what people were saying.

Moments later Libby saw Annika. Tonight the teacher wore a deep rose dress that brought soft color to her cheeks. *She's beautiful!* Libby thought. Best of all, Annika was beautiful on the inside.

Libby hurried forward and sat down next to her. "Let's save a seat for Pa." When Annika moved over, there was still an empty chair on her right, but also one on Libby's left side, next to the aisle.

To Libby's dismay her aunt Vi joined them, taking the chair on the other side of Annika. Recently Vi had come to the *Christina* for a visit. Though sisters, she and Libby's mother were very different. While her mother had loved Libby unconditionally, Vi always tried to make her over.

She still wants me to be a perfect lady, Libby thought and felt surprised that the idea no longer hurt. Only a few days before, Libby had decided she wanted to leave past hurts behind. When she forgave her aunt, Libby made a list about ways Vi had helped her.

Now Libby leaned forward to speak across Annika. "Auntie, you taught me to like music."

Vi sniffed. "I taught you to like *good* music. Look at that man's clothing! His trousers are baggy at the knees and his shirt downright ragged. What a disgrace!"

Her cheeks warm with embarrassment, Libby reminded herself that she had decided to be nice to her aunt, no matter what. *If I don't answer, maybe she'll stop talking.*

But when Pa introduced the fiddler, Vi spoke again, her voice loud enough for everyone around her to hear. "What is your father thinking of, bringing such a man into this fine group of people? Why, he might rob us before the evening is through!"

Libby slid down in her seat, trying to hide behind Annika.

Then Pa spoke in his strong, clear voice. "Tonight we have the privilege of offering some very fine music. I have the pleasure of presenting to you Mr. Franz Kadosa. Please welcome him with your applause."

Around Libby only a few people clapped, and none were enthusiastic. Libby and Annika tried to make up for the others. When Mr. Kadosa announced a sonata by Beethoven, Annika looked pleased with his choice.

As Pa sat down next to Libby, Mr. Kadosa began to play. To Libby's surprise he seemed a different person from the fiddler on the main deck. Instead of the strong rhythms of quick, bright folk tunes, he played formal classical music. Instead of attacking the strings, his bow drew long, sweet sounds. When he finished his first number, the applause started with Libby, Pa, and Annika, then grew around them.

Aunt Vi gave a few halfhearted claps. In the moment of silence before the next number, she spoke across everyone to Pa. "It's embarrassing how your violinist looks."

Pa frowned at Vi. "Mr. Kadosa wanted to play the way he was. I didn't want to rob him of that dignity." Though Pa's voice was low, even Vi understood that his words ended the matter.

When Mr. Kadosa announced his second choice, Libby had never heard of the composer. But Annika whispered, "Number

24! Very few violinists can play it!"

There was no question whether Mr. Kadosa had mastered the difficult piece. The singing tones of his violin filled the large room. By the time he finished playing a Hungarian Rhapsody, the audience no longer seemed to notice his appearance. Even Aunt Vi joined in the warm applause.

Libby felt relieved. *If Pa wants to give passengers something to think about besides the fog, he has succeeded.*

Now and then Libby caught her father watching Annika. Each time she clapped for the music, Pa looked as if he had arranged the concert just for her.

Partway through the concert, Libby noticed that something had changed. Whenever Mr. Kadosa announced a new number, he glanced around the room. At first he seemed to be making eye contact with his audience. Then Libby guessed it might be more.

Strange, she thought when she caught a pattern in what the violinist was doing. *He's careful about it. But he watches the shadows especially—the places where a man might hide.*

The idea frightened her. *I'm imagining things*, she told herself. Yet in between watching Mr. Kadosa, she stole a look at her father.

Each time Pa turned toward Libby, he could glance across the audience. Libby doubted if anyone else caught what he was doing, but she knew her father well.

When the violinist looked toward a dark corner of the room, Libby's father glanced the same way. In the midst of the next number, Mr. Kadosa turned slowly, making a circle, like he was used to playing with an audience behind him.

There's another door that way, Libby thought. *Mr. Kadosa must know that.*

Soon a man appeared from a different direction. Halfway up the cabin, between the staterooms on that side, a door opened to the deck. The man stood half in and half out of the room.

The shadows along the wall kept Libby from seeing the man's face, but Pa kept glancing that way. During intermission Libby whispered to him, "What's wrong?"

Pa's voice was so quiet that Libby had to lean close to hear. "I misunderstood," he said. "I thought Mr. Kadosa was worried about his clothes. Or that he wanted to be paid."

Now Libby felt sure about her strange uneasiness. "The fiddler has a secret," she whispered.

Pa nodded. "He's my guest. I need to protect him."

Again Pa glanced toward the door leading to the deck. As Libby's gaze followed his, she saw that no one stood there now. Yet Pa seemed just as uneasy as she felt.

"I tried to give Mr. Kadosa a stateroom, but he didn't want it," Pa said. "Tell Caleb and Jordan to make sure no one interferes with him. They should see that he returns to the main deck safely, then keep an eye on him."

While people moved about during the intermission, Libby gave Caleb and Jordan her father's message. She decided not to return to her chair. *If I'm not there, Pa can sit next to Annika.*

Soon Mr. Kadosa started playing again. Libby stood at the back of the room. At first she enjoyed the music. Then she saw that her attempt to bring Pa and Annika together had failed. Aunt Vi sat between them!

Libby groaned. *What is the matter with her?*

One guess, Libby thought. Her aunt had threatened to take Libby back to Chicago. *If Pa marries Annika, Auntie can't say I need to live with her.* The idea of living with her aunt again filled Libby with dread.

From where she stood, Libby could see the violinist even better. Everyone except Pa seemed lost in the music. Mr. Kadosa's searching had a definite pattern now.

Following the hands of a clock, he turned to the left, left center, straight ahead, right center, then right. With each turn he played enough measures to make his movements a natural part of what he was doing. As if dancing to his music, he turned around to the empty space behind him. Only his eyes gave him away, and only because Libby had seen how carefree he was with the deckers.

Near the end of the concert, Mr. Kadosa no longer turned in a circle. Each time he looked up, he faced one direction. Libby glanced that way to see what was there and saw her father looking too.

Once more the man stood near the door to the deck. Dressed

in a long black coat and hat, he seemed to melt into the shadows next to a pile of stacked chairs. Libby still could not see the man's face, only the back of his hat.

Trying not to attract attention, Libby walked back to Caleb and Jordan. "There's something bothering Mr. Kadosa," she whispered to Caleb.

When he nodded, she whispered again. "Do you see that man along the wall?"

Again Caleb nodded. "We'll take care of it."

So slowly that they seemed not to move, Caleb and Jordan separated. Both of them edged sideways, but in different directions. Caleb took the left side of the room, while Jordan moved along the right. By the time Mr. Kadosa announced his last number, Caleb stood far forward in the upper left of the room. Jordan stood close to the stack of chairs and the man in dark clothing.

Staying well back, yet close enough to see and hear, Libby followed Jordan toward the mysterious man in the shadows.

In the silence after Mr. Kadosa's last note, the audience burst into wild applause. As if to give the violinist a message, Caleb moved forward. The man in the black coat stepped from the shadows. Suddenly the heap of stacked chairs crashed to the floor in front of him.

Libby gasped. The audience turned to see what had happened. The man from the shadows turned on Jordan. "How can you be so clumsy?"

"Let me pick them up, sir," Jordan said quickly. "I'll have them out of your way in no time."

"*You* get out of my way," the man said rudely. Stepping to one side, he started around the chairs scattered across the floor. But passengers already filled the aisle.

Libby turned toward the front of the room. Mr. Kadosa was gone!

5

Safe and Free?

Soon after Libby returned to Pa, Annika, and Aunt Vi, a tall young man joined them. With light brown hair and blue eyes, he wore the finest suit of clothes that money could buy. Stretching out his hand to Pa, he introduced himself as Oliver White III.

"Captain Nathaniel Norstad," Pa replied. "What may I do for you?"

"Will you or the first lady kindly introduce me to your lovely friend?"

"The first lady?" Pa asked. It was a term often used for the captain's wife, but Pa was widowed.

"Your wife."

Pa still looked puzzled. The young man glanced toward Aunt Vi.

"Oh!" Pa said. "This is my sister-in-law, not my wife."

"I beg your pardon." Mr. White tipped his head toward Annika. "This is the young lady I would like to meet."

"Of course." Pa's mouth twitched, his eyes showing the humor of it. "I have the honor of presenting to you Miss Annika Berg."

Annika stretched out her hand, palm down. Mr. White took

it and raised it briefly to his lips. "May I have the pleasure of a walk upon the deck?"

Annika's quick glance took in Pa's face. "I'm sure that would be just fine with the captain and his first lady," she said smoothly. But her eyes held the look of mischief Libby had come to know.

The moment Annika left with Oliver White, Libby managed to escape from Aunt Vi. As she passed through the boiler deck on the way to her room, Libby saw Annika walking and talking with Mr. White. The thick fog closed in around them but hadn't spoiled Annika's enjoyment of a good time. Her laughter filled Libby with despair.

Once again the boat was tied up, and the ship's bell rang. This time the pilot, Mr. Fletcher, had managed to bring the *Christina* into the backwaters. Libby was glad to see the boat out of the main channel behind an island. "Where are we?" she asked the first deckhand she met.

"Minnesota Territory," he told her. "About eighty miles from St. Paul. Near Wabasha and Read's Landing."

On the way to her room, Libby stopped at Pa's cabin. His bed was tucked against the wall on one side. Nearby was a stand with a pitcher of water and a basin. The rest of the cabin served as a sitting room and place to bring guests when Pa needed to talk business. When necessary, the cabin also became a classroom.

Libby found her father sitting in his large rocking chair. As she sat down on the low stool beside him, he said, "One of these days you'll be so grown-up that you'll leave me."

Libby smiled. "No, Pa. Not for a long time yet."

But he was serious. "It will happen much faster than I'd like. Look how you've changed in the time since coming to live with me. You did something really special last night. In a time of danger you acted quickly and got yourself and Annika to a safer place. I want you to remember how important that was."

Pa stood up and walked over to his desk. There he opened a secret drawer and brought something out. Returning to Libby, he took her hand and laid a chain in her upturned palm.

As Libby picked up the chain, she saw a cross attached to it. The cross was small and simple, of a gold that shone in the lamplight.

"It was your mother's," Pa said. "I gave it to her when we made an important choice."

Pa stopped and waited until he could go on. When he spoke again, his voice was gruff with emotion. "Your mother knew that if we ever had a disaster on the boat, I wouldn't leave until all the passengers were off. That bothered her."

Libby swallowed hard. She could understand how her mother felt. From the time she had come on board the *Christina*, Libby had dreaded all the things that could happen to a steamboat. Already the boat named in honor of her mother had run years longer than usual. It frightened Libby that the average life of a steamboat was only five years.

"Your mother and I never wanted to be apart," Pa said. "We knew that only death would part us. In the end it was her death, not mine, that separated us. But when your mother was a young bride, afraid of being a captain's wife, we chose a symbol that would help both of us. We wanted that symbol to be the cross."

Libby felt glad that she understood. "The symbol of Jesus dying for us. He didn't have to make that choice, but He did so we can live."

Pa's smile was gentle. "Your mother made a choice to live with courage. Last night you did the same thing."

"I did?"

"I'm grateful for your quick thinking," Pa said. "Getting away from that railing in time. Pulling Annika along with you."

"It happened so fast I didn't think about it."

"That's better yet, isn't it? That you did the right thing, even without a lot of thought?"

Her throat tight with emotion, Libby looked at the cross Pa had given her. In her time on the *Christina*, she had learned what that cross meant to her personally. Now she would also see it as a symbol of the life her mother and father had together. *Their spiritual life*, Libby thought. *Besides loving each other, they shared the same beliefs*.

"Here," Pa offered. "Let me help you put it on."

When the chain hung around her neck, Libby held up the cross to look at it again. "I'll cherish it and what it means," she promised her father. "I'll cherish the double meaning."

"I knew you would," Pa said. "That's why I want you to have it."

Libby was eight when her mother died. She still longed for the talks they used to have. *Ma always knew what it meant to feel like a girl. Maybe part of me will miss Ma all my life.*

Now Libby felt strange, surprised, even. For some reason the meaning of the cross reminded her of Annika. Once, Libby had wondered why the teacher hadn't married. Annika had made it clear: *"I don't want to marry until I find a man of God who cherishes me the way I would cherish him."*

As though hearing Libby's thoughts, Pa spoke again. "I've needed all this time to grieve the loss of your mother. She would want me to go on with my life. We talked about it."

His words startled Libby. Knowing it was her fault that Pa and Annika had a bad start, Libby felt afraid to speak. More than once she had leaped into something before thinking about it. Nearly always that got her into trouble.

"Annika is a very special young woman," Pa went on. "She plans to leave the boat when we reach St. Paul. I'm trying to decide what I can do to change her mind."

"She could help you teach us," Libby said.

Pa smiled. "That's exactly my idea. Even though it's August, we'll have school again. Tell the boys to come to my cabin after breakfast. I'll ask Annika to help me."

Libby jumped up with one thought in mind. *I can hardly wait to see what happens with Pa and Annika.*

At the door Libby turned back. "Thanks, Pa." Taking hold of the chain, she lifted the small cross. Pa nodded, his eyes soft with love.

That night Libby had a hard time going to sleep. Staring up in the darkness, she kept thinking about Oliver White. *Are he and Annika still talking together? What if Annika loves him instead of Pa?*

When morning finally came, Libby dressed and went out on the hurricane deck. The fog was milky white now, and she still could not see more than a few feet beyond the front of the boat.

Finding Pa in his cabin, Libby asked about the man in the shadows.

"After you left last night, I talked with Mr. Kadosa," Pa said. "I offered to help, but he seemed afraid to talk."

"He watched the shadowman as if he didn't trust him."

"I know." Pa looked troubled. "Mr. Kadosa wouldn't explain to either Caleb or me. If he doesn't want my help, I can't force him to take it."

On the big table, Pa set out the inkwells, slates, and books they needed for school. Over the summer he had purchased the largest blackboard Libby had seen. Looking around, she remembered how she felt when she came to live on the *Christina*. At first she thought she wouldn't have to attend school. Then she discovered that Pa taught Caleb, and she would be part of that class. To Libby's surprise Caleb told her, "Your father makes learning fun."

Fun! From that moment Libby thought Caleb was strange. How could learning be fun? But Pa had gradually changed her mind. Just the same, there was one thing Libby still disliked. Pa expected them to talk about their ideas and beliefs, and Libby always wondered what Caleb would think of her. Now the class also included Jordan and Peter.

"I think you've grown at least two inches this summer," Pa told Jordan when he and Caleb came in. Already tall when he came on board the *Christina*, Jordan seemed to grow from one day to the next.

"Three inches, sir," he said respectfully. "Caleb measured me just this morning."

"We mark our height on the doorpost in Gran's kitchen," Caleb explained. "So far Jordan is winning, but I'm only an inch behind."

Terrific! Libby told herself. Five months ago she had been only one inch shorter than Caleb. Taller than most girls, Libby was glad to know he was keeping ahead of her.

Peter came in, and he and Jordan took places where they could see the blackboard. Libby and Caleb sat down on the opposite side of the table.

"I've asked Miss Berg to join us this morning," Pa said. "Here she is now."

When Annika entered the room, her gaze rested on Libby and a smile passed between them. As if seeing through Annika's eyes, Libby looked around Pa's neat cabin.

The large table used for school took up much of the room. Nearby was the desk where Pa often worked on his papers. Close to his large rocking chair were bookshelves and a small table that held Pa's open Bible.

Big windows filled the front and sides of the room. From where Libby sat, she usually watched the river flow past. Today the milk-white fog shut off any view of the water.

"Would you like to sit here?" Pa invited Annika as he placed a chair next to the blackboard.

Pa's warm smile took in all of them. "I've missed our classes this summer. A special welcome to you, Miss Berg."

Usually Pa started his teaching by reading from the Bible. This morning he turned to the eighth chapter of Romans and handed the Bible to Peter so he could read along.

Pa gave the verse from memory: " 'And we know that all things work together for good to them that love God, to them who are the called according to his purpose.' "

Then Pa bowed his head. "Thank you, Lord, that you have called us with your love. We're grateful that even when hard things happen to us, you bring something good into our lives. We ask you to build our faith and courage in you. *Amen!*"

When everyone looked up, Annika wrote quickly on the blackboard, explaining to Peter what Pa had prayed. Although Peter was teaching all of them sign language, they still had much to learn. The blackboard and the slate Peter carried in a bag over his shoulder helped them explain what they wanted to tell him.

"Before we reach St. Paul, I want to talk with you about what you're going to see," Pa said. "In 1851 the Dakota Indians signed treaties that opened up the sale of millions of acres. In just one year, 1855, over thirty thousand people arrived in Minnesota Territory. You've seen the immigrants crowd our decks and how eager they are to settle in the Territory."

Again Annika wrote quickly for Peter. Then Pa went on.

"If there's land available, there will be people to sell it. Many of them sell land at a fair price. But St. Paul also has a lot of speculators—people who take part in risky buying or selling in the hope of making a profit.

"Many people who came to Minnesota Territory bought land at a low price and sold it high. They made honest fortunes. But speculators sometimes describe land in ways that aren't true. Or they sell worthless land to people who haven't seen it."

Annika wrote *worthless land* and drew a frowning face.

"Now," Pa said, "if an area is overflowing with new settlers, what do you think will happen?"

"Minnesota Territory will become a state," Caleb said.

Pa nodded. "Because St. Paul is the territory's capital, you might see people working to make the territory a state. You might see some of the difficult things that happen in a changing area. But you'll also meet good people who want to carve out a new life on the frontier. Or people who want to help others shape their lives into something good."

"People such as Harriet Bishop." Annika's eyes shone with excitement.

"I haven't met Miss Bishop," Pa answered. "But I hear that she cares deeply about what happens to people. When the city was new, she put up with a lot of hardship in order to teach children."

Pa looked around the room. "During our time in St. Paul, think about the speculators, the immigrants, the people who want to build a new state. Do they have a dream of life, liberty, and the pursuit of happiness? What do they want? But first, think about your own beliefs."

In large letters Pa put his questions on the board:

What is most important to you? What do you want?

"Write your answer in one sentence," Pa told them. "Write it on your slate, then on a piece of paper you can keep."

At first the room was silent, as everyone thought about their answers. Libby searched her mind, trying to think what to say. It would be easy for Caleb. He wanted to be a newspaperman— a reporter or editor. More than once he had said so. But it was a different matter deciding for herself.

Pa knows I want a never-give-up family. And I can't say that I want

Pa and Annika to get married. Libby's face burned with shame as she remembered her words to Annika after a threat from Aunt Vi. *"If you and Pa got married, I wouldn't have to go back to Chicago."* Since Annika hadn't even met Pa, she didn't appreciate Libby's help.

Then Libby remembered her fear in the fog. She knew what to do.

Soon the silence was broken by the sound of slate pencils and Jordan speaking softly to Annika. While a slave, Jordan hadn't been allowed to learn how to read or write. In the months since reaching freedom, he had made great leaps in what he knew. Yet he still needed help in writing, and Annika put down what he wanted to say.

After a time Pa went to the board, pointed to his questions, then to Peter to tell him, "Let's start with you."

"I want to be an explorer, and I want to help people," Peter answered. "All of you have been helping me. Now I want to help *you.*"

Tears welled up in Libby's eyes. For Peter, being an orphan had not only meant having no family. The man Peter lived with after his family died had been dishonest and cruel.

Leaning forward, Libby signed words Peter had taught her. "Little brother." Then she changed one word to show how much she liked his answer. "*Big* brother."

"Jordan," Pa said. "What about you?"

"I need to know what to tell my family about St. Paul."

"You'd better explain what you mean." Pa hadn't had a chance to talk with Jordan since leaving Galena.

"My brother, Zack, keeps pestering my momma and daddy," Jordan said. "Zack says, 'Are we really safe now?' So Momma and Daddy have been talkin'. Before I left for St. Paul, they told me, 'Jordan, you go spy out the land. Take a look around and see if that's a place where we can live in freedom.' "

Pa nodded. "St. Paul might be just exactly what your family needs."

But it might not, Libby thought. *What if someone from the South recognizes Jordan or his family?*

"So," Pa said, "there's something even bigger than knowing

the place where you should live."

"Yessuh. All our lives we have been wantin' to go to Canada. All the years we were slaves, that was the Promised Land—the place where we could be free at last. But two nights ago Daddy said, 'If we go to Canada we be leavin' this country. Maybe we need to be helpin' other slaves who want to start a new life. If we stay here, we can help make this country a place where us colored folk live free.' So I want to find a place where my family can live safe and free."

"I'll be in St. Paul longer than usual," Pa told Jordan. "It will give you a few days to look around."

Pa looked at Libby. "Your turn. What are you thinking?"

Just then Libby saw beyond Pa to the window. In that moment she forgot everything else.

What was it? A person? Did someone look in, then step back out of sight?

6

Hated Drawing

*E*ven to herself, Libby couldn't explain what had happened. One question stayed in her thoughts: Was someone trying to listen in?

"Hey, Libby!" Caleb waved his hand in front of her face. "We're here, you know, not out there." He tipped his head toward the windows.

Libby gulped as she realized everyone was waiting for her. When she spoke, Libby stumbled over her words. "I want to be strong."

Caleb snickered. "But you *are* strong. Stronger than any girl I know!"

Libby glared at him. *Giving a boy a bloody nose wasn't quite what I had in mind.*

Then a big fear popped into her head. *Caleb Whitney, don't you dare tell Pa what I did!*

"What do you mean by being strong?" Pa asked.

Now Libby was doing exactly what she didn't want—having to talk about her feelings in front of everybody. But she had no choice. "I want to be able to handle things, even when they're hard."

"I'm glad, Libby." Pa's smile warmed her heart. "Being strong is something every one of us needs."

Pa turned to Caleb. "What did you decide?"

Libby waited, expecting Caleb to talk about being a news-paperman. When he spoke Caleb's voice was quiet but sure. "I want to know God better."

Know God better? Libby couldn't believe her ears. *Aw, come on, Caleb. How can you say something like that—something so big and important—in front of everyone?*

For a moment Pa was so moved that he couldn't speak. Finally he said, "Caleb, of all the things you might want, that is the very best."

As Pa looked around the room, his gaze stopped at each of them. "I suspect all of us want to know God better, and we don't know how to say it."

That's for sure. Libby liked Caleb. She especially liked what he stood for, but sometimes he seemed so . . .

Libby tried to think what it was. *So spiritual.* Sometimes Libby wondered if Caleb was real—why he didn't do the kind of stupid things she always stumbled into. It was scary to see someone her age do things so well.

For a time they worked on their lessons. Then Pa asked them to listen again. "It's important that each of you know what you want in life. What you care about most will shape everything you do. That's why I need to tell you something.

"Because you decided what you want most—what you believe in—you might have a time of testing. All kinds of things can happen that make you wonder if you made the right choice. You might even think, 'Do I really believe what I said?'

"If that happens, you need to make another choice. Are you going to throw away what you care about—to say it doesn't matter? Or will you decide it *does* matter, and you're going to stick to what you believe? That's when you need to ask God to help you."

Libby's stomach tightened. It sounded too much like a hard assignment in school. *I don't want to be tested.*

As if hearing her thoughts, Pa spoke again. "Let God wrap His arms of love around you."

Libby knew what that meant. Letting God love her was like

being a little girl again. Having Pa hold her on his lap. Or feeling Ma's arms around her, even when she felt afraid.

I can handle that, Libby decided. Crossing her arms over her chest, Libby hugged herself to remember God's love. In that moment her fear disappeared.

When Annika finished writing for Peter, she looked at Pa. The concern in his eyes didn't go away.

Then Peter spoke up. "We should have a secret mark."

"What do you mean?" Pa signed.

"You know how the early Christians helped each other?"

Pa knew, but he let Peter tell them. "When I was little, Mama and Papa told me how Christians hid in the catacombs of Rome. Other people were scared to go there because that's where people were buried. But Christians weren't scared. They were safe there. And they had a secret sign."

With two quick strokes, Peter drew a simple fish on the blackboard. "The early Christians spoke a different language than we do." He explained that the five letters in their word for fish stood for five words: Jesus Christ, God's Son, Savior. The fish helped Christians recognize one another.

Pa's smile was gentle. Careful to not spoil the fish Peter had drawn, Pa wrote on the board, "Your mother and father taught you well, Peter."

"It can be our secret signal," Peter insisted. "When we draw a fish, it means that one of us has been there."

But Libby felt uneasy again, even afraid. She didn't like Peter's game. It seemed too serious, too much like something they might need to use.

Once more she looked toward the windows. Just then something caught her attention. Something half seen out of the corner of her eye.

Libby glanced toward Caleb, then realized that Pa blocked Caleb's view of the window. *What is it? How can there be a shadow with the fog hiding the sun?*

Libby jumped up and hurried over to the window. When she looked out, there was no one in sight. Trying to cover up her strange move, she turned and pretended she was helping Annika.

But later as they left Pa's cabin, Caleb asked, "What was wrong with you? It's like you were half here, half not here."

"You think so, huh?" Embarrassed again, Libby put away her plan of telling Caleb what was wrong. Not for anything would she do it now. "Maybe I saw more than all of you!"

Standing at the railing with Caleb, Libby turned her back to him. At least things had gone well with Annika. *If she wants to marry a man of God, she sure would have one with Pa.*

Then Libby remembered. *Pa didn't tell us what he wants.* That was all right because Libby thought she knew. *But what does Annika want?*

Again Libby felt uneasy. *A time of testing ahead? Pa never goes looking for trouble. He wouldn't warn us unless he thought it was important.*

Libby drew a deep breath and felt a gentle wind touch her arms. The breeze was blowing the fog away. As the sun appeared, she noticed a small stream flowing into the backwaters. Then the *Christina*'s engines started, and Libby heard the flutter of wings. Two large, dark brown birds flew up from along the creek.

"They're eagles!" Caleb exclaimed. When he pushed the blond hair out of his eyes, Libby knew her anger about his teasing was gone.

As the eagles spread their great wings, Libby saw their white heads and tail feathers. Rising higher and higher, the eagles soared against the bright blue sky. Libby watched until they disappeared from sight.

"I wish I could fly like that," she said softly.

Just as softly came Caleb's answer. "You can. That's your pa's verse."

Libby looked at him, not understanding. *What do you mean, Caleb?* she wanted to ask.

When he didn't say more, Libby thought about it. *All things work together for good to them that love God?*

Like a stream of living water, the words flowed through Libby's mind. Again she wondered, *What does that mean? I love you, God. So that means the promise is for me. But what does it really mean? How can I fly like an eagle? Soar up in the clouds?*

Then Libby put her questions aside. *If something hard comes, I'll figure it out. Right now I want to remember this day, this moment, these eagles soaring up and away.*

Her wish during class became a prayer. *Help me be strong, Lord. Even if hard times come, help me remember that you love me, that you can bring something good.*

After lunch Libby found Caleb, Jordan, and Peter on the main deck. She also noticed Mr. Kadosa. "There's the fiddler," Libby said. "Let's go talk to him."

The musician sat on a large crate near the edge of the deck, looking out over the river. Libby walked up behind him. "Mr. Kadosa?"

When he did not turn, Libby raised her voice. "Mr. Kadosa?" Still the fiddler paid no attention.

Is he hard of hearing? Libby wondered. Not wanting to touch his arm or shoulder the way she would with Peter, Libby walked around in front of the fiddler. "Mr. Kadosa?" she said again, facing him now.

The fiddler jerked to attention. "Good afternoon!" he said, greeting her warmly.

For the first time Libby saw his face in the sunlight, and he looked younger than she thought. Just below the jawbone on the left side of his neck was a small area of red, roughened skin from the chin rest of his violin.

"I'm Libby," she said. "Captain Norstad's daughter." She pointed to each of the boys. "Caleb Whitney. Jordan Parker. Peter Christopherson. We want to thank you for your wonderful concerts."

"Concerts?" he asked. "More than one?"

"We heard both of them. The one on the deck and the one in the main cabin."

"Tell me," the fiddler said. "Which one did you like best?"

Libby smiled. "The one on the deck."

Mr. Kadosa smiled too. "I gave to them the fun."

Just then Peter moved forward. "Do you have a family?"

When Mr. Kadosa started to answer, Peter held out his slate. "Please. I can't hear."

Taking the slate pencil, the fiddler began to write. "I have a boy as nice as you, but he is younger." Mr. Kadosa held up his hand and spread his fingers wide.

"Five years old," Peter said.

The fiddler nodded, then erased his words on the slate and wrote again. "I teach him to play the violin. He makes many screeches."

Mr. Kadosa held his hands over his ears and made a face. Peter laughed.

"But my son will learn," Mr. Kadosa wrote. "He will learn as I learned." Pointing to himself, the fiddler forgot to write. "He become gut."

Good, Libby thought. *Mr. Kadosa's son will become a good fiddler*.

"Please," Mr. Kadosa said as Libby and the boys started to leave. "Call me Franz."

Strange, Libby told herself. *I know Mr. Kadosa is a concert violinist. Probably the best violinist I'll ever meet. But I heard him first as a fiddler, and that's how I think of him.*

Even so, Libby felt more puzzled than ever. She had wondered if the fiddler had a secret. Now he didn't seem mysterious after all.

When Libby went to her room, she found Samson lying in one of his favorite places, right outside her door. From five months of experience, Libby knew that sometimes Samson parted his mouth in a grin and said "Wooof!" from deep in his throat. By contrast, Wellington was a yappy little dog.

As Peter followed Libby up the stairs, his terrier followed him. With one look at Samson, Wellington stiffened. In the next instant, he planted his four spindly legs for battle. At the terrier's sharp bark, Samson lifted his head.

Wellington backed away, then danced around to one side of the large Newfoundland. Samson turned his head, and the small dog started barking in earnest. *Yap, yap, yap!*

Still watching the terrier, Samson stood up. That made Libby nervous. "Hold your dog!" she told Peter, then remembered he couldn't hear.

But Peter seemed worried, too, and scooped Wellington up in his arms. A minute later the terrier jumped free. Landing on the deck, he took up his battle position. Circling Samson, he yapped with every move.

Just then Caleb and Jordan came up the stairs. "What's going on?" Caleb asked.

Seeing the small dog stand off against the big one, Jordan grinned. "I'm bettin' on Wellington."

"No!" Libby exclaimed, unwilling to believe her dog could lose. "Samson's being careful. He doesn't want to hurt Wellington."

At that Caleb laughed. "How many for Wellington? How many for Samson?"

Planting his four paws, Samson lifted his head. From deep in his throat came a low *woooof!*

Wellington backed away. Looking relieved, Peter glanced at Libby. Just then the terrier ran straight for Samson.

Samson stood his place. As the terrier circled around him, Samson waited. But his head moved left to right, and his eyes followed the smaller dog.

Yap, yap, yap!

Again Samson raised his head. Backing away, Wellington faced his opponent.

Samson waited. Once more the smaller dog rushed in. Suddenly Samson put one giant paw on Wellington's back and pushed the small dog to the deck.

Instantly the terrier's barking changed to whimpers. As Wellington yelped and squirmed, Samson held him there.

After a moment Samson lifted his paw. Wellington yipped again, leaped up, and scampered away.

When Peter caught him, the little dog shivered and tucked his nose into the crook of Peter's elbow. The next time Wellington lifted his head, he did not bark at Samson.

Later that afternoon Libby took out her pencils and drawing paper. While living in Chicago, she had taken lessons from a famous artist. Whenever she could, Libby practiced. Now she perched on top of a barrel and sketched deckers. She started with the children, then drew a mother or father.

Remembering Pa's school lesson, Libby looked for immigrants. Often they wore a piece of paper pinned to their shirt or dress. The paper helped other people tell an immigrant when to get off a boat or train.

As Libby drew, she listened. *What do they want?* she asked herself. *What do they* really *want?* Often Libby couldn't understand enough of their language to know.

She was hard at work when she heard a rude voice. "Hey, there!" Libby looked up to see Jordan crossing the deck.

"You, boy!" the man called.

Jordan froze. His shoulders stiff, his face gone blank, he turned to see who was calling.

A short, thin man stood behind him. With his hair slicked down and his collar high around his chin, he seemed to have no neck. But he spit out his words as if he owned the whole world.

Then the man's eyes widened with surprise. "I know *you*! You're Micah Parker's son."

For one instant Jordan cringed. Then, almost without drawing a breath, he straightened, standing tall. "Yessuh, I am Micah Parker's son," he answered respectfully. "And proud of it."

"Then you better run scared because I'm going to tell your owner where you are!"

Jordan's fists tightened. "You sayin' I should run scared?" As his gaze locked on to the man's eyes, Jordan leaned forward, hovering over the shorter man.

Suddenly the man stepped back. He wasted no time leaving, but Jordan's words followed him.

"Tell my owner where I is. And tell him I am *not* afraid. Tell him I be Micah Parker's son, and I is not livin' scared!"

As the short, thin man disappeared, Libby smiled. In that moment Jordan had forgotten all the fine English he had worked so hard to learn. But he hadn't forgotten who he was.

Then Libby remembered Pa's warning, and her good feelings faded. Jordan had passed the first test, but Libby couldn't help but wonder if there were more ahead.

After a while she walked up the wide stairway to the area on

the boiler deck where first-class passengers took their exercise. In a shaded, out-of-the-way place, Libby sat down.

Soon her gaze rested on a man who stood alone. Though he leaned over the railing, peering down at the water, Libby could see most of his brown hair and the right side of his face. With quick lines she started to sketch.

When she finished the drawing, Libby realized it was good— very good. She had tried to be honest in showing the hard lines around the man's mouth. His face rang a warning bell in Libby's mind. *Is there something wrong in his life?*

Just then the man glanced her way and saw her pencils and paper. His eyes darkened with anger.

In the next instant Libby pulled other pages over the sketch, but it was too late. The man knew she had drawn his picture. For some reason that upset him.

Libby gathered up her pencils, got to her feet, and walked away. At a wall that would hide her from sight, she glanced back. Whoever the man was, he still watched her.

In spite of the warm day, Libby felt cold all over. *Who is he?* she wondered again. *Is he a crook and afraid he'll be recognized?* The expression in his hard face frightened her.

Mr. Trouble, that's what I'd call him.

7

Where Is It?

*L*ibby went straight to the *Christina*'s office. "I'd like to put one of my drawings in the safe," she told the young clerk who worked there. As he opened the safe, he looked curious but made no comment.

He doesn't dare ask why, Libby thought, wanting to giggle. *He knows I'm the captain's daughter.*

By the time she finished eating the evening meal, the sun had dropped low in the western sky. Libby went to her room in the texas, the boxlike structure near the top of the boat where many crew members had their rooms. Long shadows fell across her bed, but Libby could still see her way around.

The first thing she noticed was that her drawings were out of order. Then she knew someone had opened her large trunk. Next she found a drop of wax on the floor. Here on the texas, far away from water and help, Pa did not allow her to use a candle. Yet there was no mistaking the wax.

Someone was here while I was gone. Someone entered my room, my private place. Whoever that person is, he looked through my things, searched everything I own. It has to be the man I saw on deck!

At first Libby felt angry. She wanted to scream, to cry out, to sob. *That man wanted the sketch I drew. Why? Who is he? What is he trying to hide?*

Then Libby knew something even worse. *Whoever he is, he knows I can recognize him. That I can show the drawing to others.*

Without wasting another moment, Libby went looking for her father. She found him and Annika sitting on the hurricane deck, talking together. Libby stopped, not wanting to break in.

Annika saw her and asked, "What's wrong, Libby?"

When she finished telling them, Pa had another question. "Do you know the man's name?"

Libby shook her head. "He looked like Mr. Trouble to me."

"Give me his description again."

"Tall, brown hair, blue eyes. Cruel lines around his mouth." Libby told about the drawing in the safe.

"I'll get my best men working on it," Pa said. "We haven't much time before we reach St. Paul. But if they see the drawing, they can begin to search."

Pa started off, then came back. "I love you, Libby," he said. "Remember that, okay? Bring your blankets to my cabin tonight. You can make a bed on the floor."

Partway across the deck, Pa turned back a second time. "That man has it in for you, Libby. Wherever you go, take Samson along."

"I wonder what's going on," Libby said to Annika after Pa left. "First, the man in the shadows. Then the one who threatened Jordan. Now the man who searched my room." Just thinking about it, Libby's stomach knotted again.

"Maybe it's like children in a classroom," Annika said. "If they're troublemakers, they always manage to find each other."

"You mean they've found each other on the *Christina*? And we can expect more trouble?"

"Maybe," Annika said. "Your pa would know better than I."

Half an hour later, Libby and Peter watched from the hurricane deck as the *Christina* rounded the bend a mile below St. Paul. As the steamboat whistled its long, deep blast, Libby saw the city against the last rose color of the sunset.

Near the riverfront stood large warehouses. On higher ground homes and businesses spread across the bluff. Rising above all the other buildings, church steeples pointed upward. Then a high, squealing noise shattered the peace. As the bloodcurdling sound cut through to her bones, Libby trembled. *Is this what it means to come to Minnesota Territory?*

When she turned to Peter, his happy look had not changed. But Wellington yipped and squirmed, rubbing his paws against his ears.

The high-pitched squeal kept on and on. Unlike anything Libby had ever heard, the sound terrified her. Leaping up, she ran to her father's cabin.

"It's the Red River oxcarts," he said, meeting her at the door. "Don't be afraid."

"Oxcarts?" Libby whirled around. Ahead, she could see nothing but an island and the buildings on the bluffs.

"Two-wheeled carts filled with furs," Pa explained. "They come from Pembina, way up at the edge of Minnesota Territory, near the Canadian border. The drivers don't use grease on the axles. It's wood turning on wood. People say they hear the squeal for miles."

Libby believed it. Though she couldn't see the carts, the noise was so loud that Pa had to talk above it.

Going to the railing, he stared upstream. "Usually the drivers reach St. Paul in July. I wonder why they're here now?"

Pa turned to leave. "There might be a hundred carts or more. I need to talk to the passengers. They'll be frightened too."

Libby went back to Peter. By now the *Christina* was close enough for them to see the steamboat landing. Peter still tried to hold Wellington in his arms, but the dog wiggled and squirmed, yipping continually.

"What's wrong with him?" Peter asked.

Libby pointed to the dog's ears, made a face showing pain, then covered her own ears with her hands.

"Do you have an earache?" Peter asked. "Does Wellington have an earache?"

Libby took Peter's slate. "Oxcarts," she wrote. "High squeal. Hurts Wellington's ears. Mine too."

Libby motioned toward the streets of St. Paul. "Watch," she signed. "Maybe we'll see them."

Four other steamboats had already tied up at the Lower Landing. Mr. Fletcher, the pilot, guided the *Christina* to the flat area of land that was the levee.

Beyond the waterfront a dirt street led up the steep bluff. There Libby saw the oxcarts pass by. Their wheels were huge— five feet high or so. The drivers walked beside their oxen.

As the *Christina*'s deckhands threw out the lines, Libby hurried down to the main deck to watch. She found Caleb standing near where the gangplank would go down. His gun told Libby that he, too, was eager to visit St. Paul.

The line of first-class passengers waiting to go on shore backed up the stairway. Near the steps on the side away from the gangplank, Oliver White stood along the wall. On the deck next to him was his large trunk.

I wonder how he got back there, Libby thought, surprised that he hadn't pushed his way to the head of the line. Then Libby saw that Mr. White was talking with Annika.

Uh-oh! Libby thought. *I hope they aren't becoming friends.* She disliked even the thought.

The squeal of oxcarts went on and on. Then, to Libby's relief, it finally stopped. Through the opening between warehouses, she saw men start to unload their carts.

The moment the *Christina*'s gangplank went out, the first-class passengers streamed across. Waiting their turn, deckers stood with baggage ready and children in hand. The tired, worn look Libby had often seen on the immigrants' faces was gone. Instead, their eyes were full of hope, their voices eager. The sound of several languages filled the air.

In the long twilight after sunset, a man carried a young boy across the gangplank. Once clear of the crowd, the man set the boy on his feet and pointed down.

"Minnesota Territory," he said. "Sure and if we aren't in the land of opportunity." Dropping to his knees, the man kissed the ground. His son dropped down beside him.

Libby couldn't imagine herself kneeling in the dirt, touching her lips to the trampled soil of the landing. Yet as she looked around, a woman did the same thing. When she rose to her feet again, excitement lit her face.

I've never really understood, Libby thought. *With both Pa and Auntie, I've always had a home, a safe place.*

Forgetting everything else, Libby watched the people leave the *Christina*. Young and old. Single and married. Couples with no children. Parents with few or many children. Some with little baggage, others with much. All with one look. They were eager to begin a new life.

The fiddler stood among them. Waiting in line, Franz held a carpetbag in one hand and his violin case in the other. Ahead of him a woman with two children balanced a large cloth bag on her shoulder. In spite of the warm evening, she wore a heavy black coat.

As she started onto the gangplank, the woman reached down, took the hand of the youngest child, and motioned for the other girl to follow. Halfway across the gangplank, the older girl looked down at the dark water and froze.

Caleb started over to help, but Franz set his belongings on a crate and hurried forward. Taking the child's hand, he led her safely across.

Other immigrants streamed forward. Out of the corner of her eye, Libby caught a quick movement. Then the crowd shifted, and Libby saw Franz again.

"Tank you, tank you," the woman said as she reached the levee.

"You'll be fine now?" he asked. "You have someone to meet you?"

"Yah, my husband, he meet me here." The woman pointed to the piece of paper pinned to her coat. It read *St. Paul, Minnesota Territory*. "My husband, he come here to work, save money to bring us to America." She touched the blond hair of the youngest child. "This one he has never seen."

Franz wished the woman well and hurried back across the gangplank to the *Christina*. When he reached the crate where he had left his violin and carpetbag, his smile disappeared. Suddenly he cried out. "My violin! It is gone!"

As Libby whirled around, a tall man slipped through the door into the cargo room.

"Caleb!" Libby called, and the two tore after him. In the dimly lit area they raced between piles of freight, following the sound of running footsteps.

Before long the footsteps stopped. Libby and Caleb stopped to listen. From one side of the boat, Libby heard a door close.

Caleb leaped into action. Libby followed him through the cargo area to the engine room. On the far side Caleb flung open the door. When he and Libby came out on the side deck, it was empty.

They raced along the deck toward the front of the boat. When Caleb rounded the corner, he stopped so suddenly that Libby crashed into him. Together they scanned the crowd of immigrants still waiting to leave. Not one person moved quickly, as though trying to flee.

Caleb frowned. "Whoever that thief is, he's mighty bold."

"Did you see his face?" Libby asked.

Neither of them had managed to get a good look. Angry at his failure to catch the man, Caleb pounded his fist against his hand.

To Libby's relief Annika was no longer talking to Oliver White. He still stood next to his trunk, waiting for the crowded front deck to clear. Looking concerned, he asked, "Did you find anything?"

Caleb shook his head. Moving between the deckers, he and Libby made their way over to Franz.

"Where is it?" he asked. "Where is my violin?"

8

The Pawnshop

"*I*t is my work!" the fiddler cried. "The way I earn my living. But it is more!"

Growing more frantic by the minute, Mr. Kadosa ran his fingers through his hair. "From one father to the next my violin has come. Now I teach it to my son. It is—" He paused to think of the word. "It is great value."

"Very valuable," Caleb said.

Suddenly the fiddler broke into a language Libby didn't recognize. Just as suddenly he broke off to speak in English. "I come to America because people said it is the land of opportunity. I say it is the land of thieves!"

"Oh no!" Libby exclaimed. "Because one man steals doesn't mean everyone steals. When one person does something wrong, it doesn't mean everyone will treat you that way!"

Libby thought of the cruel slave catchers who wanted the reward on Jordan's head. Yet a slave owner's wife had tried to protect Jordan's family.

"Even if a whole group of people is unkind, it doesn't mean everyone in our country is unkind," Libby went on. "No matter where you go—north, east, south, west—there are good people."

His eyes filled with pain, the fiddler shook his head. "Wherever I go people ask me how long I have played the violin. I can't remember. I was the age of my son when I stood on a chair to play. And now it is gone. All gone!"

"Maybe not," Caleb said. "We need to go to the police."

"The police?" The fiddler's eyes filled with fear. "Nein! Not the police!"

For a moment Caleb stood there thinking. "In America the police are friends to good people," he said. "The police will help us."

The fiddler shook his head. "Nein, nein, nein!"

"The police will help us find your violin."

"Nein, nein, nein!"

"We're wasting time," Caleb answered. "We need to catch the thief at once. Come with us to the police. You don't have to go in. I'll talk to them."

Still looking uneasy, Franz followed Caleb across the levee. When they reached the police station, the fiddler waited outside with Libby.

Soon Caleb returned. "I did my best," he told Franz. "But I don't know if they'll find your violin."

From the police station they walked to the *Pioneer and Democrat* newspaper office. There they found someone working late. Caleb helped the fiddler place an ad offering a reward for the return of his violin.

"We can't do any more tonight," Caleb told the fiddler as they started back to the Lower Landing. "All the shops are closed. Tomorrow Libby and I will help you search."

Near the river the streets became more and more crowded. It seemed that every spare inch of ground had been taken. Many immigrants had turned the tops of their trunks into tables. One family had stretched canvas between two barrels to make a roof.

Seeing the small shelters in which people lived and slept upset Libby. "People are living in the streets!"

"When navigation opened in May, three thousand people arrived in four days," Caleb said. "It's kept up all summer."

"But soon winter will come!" Libby knew that many people would pass into the countryside and begin to farm. Yet she felt sure that others wanted to stay and find work in the city.

"Hotels and boardinghouses are filled to overflowing," Caleb told her. "Even if people have the money to pay, there's nowhere in St. Paul to go."

It wasn't hard to figure out that Franz needed a place to spend the night. "Come back to the *Christina* with us," Libby invited. "I'll ask Pa if you can live on the boat till we leave. We'll help you find your violin."

Early the next morning, Libby stood on the main deck, waiting for the gangplank to go down. When Caleb, Jordan, and Peter joined her, Wellington came along.

The minute the deckhands put out the gangplank, Wellington tore across. Samson raced after him, following the smaller dog up Jackson Street.

At first Libby didn't worry about the dogs running ahead. Whenever they left the boat, they needed exercise. Stopping here and there to look around, Caleb and Jordan took their time in following. When the dogs got farther and farther away, Libby hurried to catch up. She didn't trust Wellington.

Before long the terrier headed down a side street. Reaching an area of homes and fenced-in yards, Wellington scared up a rabbit. Dodging this way and that, the rabbit fled under a boardwalk. Pushing his nose into the hole, Wellington yapped until the rabbit ran out the other side.

Again the dog took up the chase. When Peter called him back, Wellington didn't obey. Upset now, Libby faced Peter, pointed to the dog, and signed her strongest "No!"

A moment later the rabbit disappeared under a white picket fence. Wellington burrowed under the fence after him. Samson came to a halt and peered between the pickets.

Along one side of the house, the rabbit raced to a small vegetable garden. When he disappeared, Wellington sniffed his way after him until the rabbit bounded off. This time he got away.

Libby breathed a sigh of relief. But when Peter called, Wellington still didn't obey. Off again, he burrowed his nose in the dirt of the garden.

"What's wrong with your dog?" Libby signed.

"He knows how to drive game from holes in the ground," Peter answered proudly. "He's just doing what is natural for him."

"Well, teach him to do what *isn't* natural!" Libby said, then felt glad that Peter hadn't heard. By comparison, Samson was a model dog.

Now Wellington was digging. As dirt flew out behind his paws, Peter opened the gate and raced into the yard. When he tried to pick up the dog, Wellington leaped away.

Uh-oh! Libby thought, but this time even Peter was upset. Already Wellington was digging another big hole. As the mound of dirt rose behind the dog, Peter grabbed him.

While Peter held the dog in his arms, Libby filled in the holes. Soon her hands and feet were covered with dirt. When she finished, she could be glad for only one thing. At least the terrier hadn't broken off any plants.

Then Libby discovered that Samson was gone. Hurrying out of the garden, she looked up and down the street. Farther down

the block, Caleb and Jordan were watching a man build a large house. His mouth stretched wide in a grin, Samson sat on his haunches beside them.

As Libby and Peter caught up, Jordan spoke to the carpenter on the ladder.

"You want to talk with me, son?" the man asked as he climbed down.

"Will you tell me what it's like for our people to live in Minnesota Territory?" Jordan asked.

The man offered his hand. "I'm James Thompson."

"Jordan Parker."

"Been here long, Jordan?" Mr. Thompson asked.

"Came into St. Paul yesterday. What about you?"

Mr. Thompson smiled. "Since a long while before you were born. A Methodist missionary needed an interpreter with the Indians, and I started working for him. He bought my papers and set me free."

Mr. Thompson slipped his hammer through a loop in his overalls and sat down on a keg of nails. "Do I like living in St. Paul? Yes, I do. I like building houses here. Have you seen how crowded it is?"

Jordan nodded. "People livin' in the streets. But someone said if there's money, a man can build a house in a day."

"A shack in a day," Mr. Thompson answered. "Not the kind of houses I build. In winter the wind blows straight down from the north. The cold goes right into your bones. My houses keep people warm."

Mr. Thompson looked Jordan in the eyes. "Why do you ask about Minnesota Territory?"

"I want a place where my momma and my daddy and my sisters and my brother can live safe and free. If we have to be cold, we'll be cold, but will we be free?"

Mr. Thompson met Jordan's gaze straight on. "Living in Minnesota Territory is like living anywhere. If you let yourself be free, you will be."

That's a strange answer, Libby thought. She felt sure Mr. Thompson wasn't telling Jordan to do whatever he pleased. *What does he mean?*

"Are you free to live?" Mr. Thompson asked.

Jordan nodded. "Free to earn my own way. Free to read and write."

"Free to vote?"

Jordan drew himself up. "Now you're makin' fun of me. There isn't any colored man who votes."

Mr. Thompson smiled. "Not yet, but that's part of what the problem in St. Paul is about. The Democrats and Republicans are supposed to be writing a state constitution together. Instead, they're so upset with each other, they're meeting in separate conventions. The new Republican Party wants to give us colored men the right to vote."

Jordan stepped back, staring. "Mr. Thompson, I don't want to be disrespectful like. But are you telling me the truth?"

"I'm telling you, those Republicans in St. Paul are working on it. I don't know if they'll get it. If they don't come to a compromise with the Democrats, Minnesota Territory won't become a state."

Jordan shook his head, still not believing. "Mr. Thompson, five months ago I ran away from my master. Five months ago these friends of mine started teachin' me to read and write."

Jordan glanced toward Caleb and Libby. "And five months ago I earned my first nickel. You look like an honest man, Mr. Thompson, but havin' the right to vote is mighty hard to believe."

Mr. Thompson's smile reached his eyes. "Jordan, when I offered my hand, you took it. Were you trusting me then?"

As Jordan nodded, his gaze clung to the man's face.

Again Mr. Thompson offered his hand. Without blinking, Jordan met it with his. A wide grin spread across his face.

"What's your daddy good at?" Mr. Thompson asked.

"He's the best man with horses you'll ever find." Jordan's voice was sure and strong. "People say, 'Why, that Micah Parker, there ain't a horse alive that he can't ride. There ain't a horse *anywhere* that he can't train.' And they're right!"

"If you want to bring your family here, look for work," Mr. Thompson said. "A number of our people work at the Winslow House."

"In St. Paul?" Jordan asked.

"There are two hotels called the Winslow House. One in St. Paul, and one about ten miles from here in St. Anthony. That's the hotel I'm talking about. Some of the people who work there live at Fort Snelling. Others live in the basement of the hotel till they build their own houses."

"Build their own houses?" Jordan's voice was filled with awe.

"And, Jordan, there are seven colored families starting a church."

Jordan straightened in the tall, proud look that reminded Libby of royalty. "My momma and my daddy, my sister Serena, my brother, Zack, my little sister Rose, and me—" Excitement filled Jordan's eyes and face. "We could be the eighth family!"

"Hope to see you sometime," Mr. Thompson said as he started back up the ladder. "Till then, let yourself be free."

Again Libby wondered what he meant. But as they left Mr. Thompson, Jordan said, "I just got a taste of freedom that makes me want to do my best in everything!"

When Libby and the boys returned to the *Christina*, they found the fiddler waiting for them.

"I think the pawnshop will be open by now," Caleb told him. "The thief might go there. It's a good place to get rid of something stolen."

Peter decided to stay behind. "I need to help your pa," he told Libby. "He said I could be his cabin boy." Peter made it sound so important that Libby felt curious.

As they set out, Caleb explained to Franz and Jordan that a pawnshop was a place where people borrowed money. If a man needed a loan, the pawnbroker would give that man the money in exchange for something to prove he'd pay the pawnbroker back.

"If I had a watch," Caleb said, "I'd give it to him. But the pawnbroker wouldn't give me what it's worth. He would also charge high interest. If I couldn't pay up, I wouldn't get my watch back."

"I know what you mean," Jordan said. "A thief sells something for less than it's worth. But he makes enough money to keep on stealin'."

Caleb grinned. "You got it!"

As they entered the shop, a bell on the door jangled. The pawnshop was a large, dimly lit room with two closed doors along the right side. On the opposite side was a rack of coats. Nearby, a glass case held watches and jewelry. The back half of the room was closed off to customers by a wall that looked like a metal cage.

When a short, thin man came out from behind the cage, Libby stared at him. With his hair slicked down and his collar high, the man seemed to have no neck.

Trying to think why he seemed familiar, Libby stepped back while Caleb asked questions. Like Libby, Franz looked around, and Jordan stared through the cagelike wall.

"A man trying to sell a fiddle stopped by just a few minutes ago," the pawnbroker said in answer to Caleb's questions. "He didn't think I offered him enough money, so he left."

"What did the man look like?" Libby asked quickly.

"Tall. Blue eyes. Blond hair like his." The man tipped his head toward Caleb.

Glancing beyond him, the pawnbroker caught sight of Jordan just as he looked up. When their gazes met, Jordan stepped back as he recognized the man. In that instant Libby knew who the pawnbroker was.

The man on the Christina *who threatened Jordan! The man who knows Jordan is Micah Parker's son!*

9

Mr. Trouble

*W*ithin three seconds Jordan was out the door. The rest of them caught up two blocks away. Jordan stood out of sight behind a building, waiting for them to come past.

"If that man knows I'm Micah Parker's son, who else does he know in St. Paul?" Jordan asked as they walked back to the *Christina*.

Libby was upset. "He said he knows Riggs. But we don't know where Riggs is."

Of one thing Libby felt sure. "That pawnbroker is evil all the way through. I'm sure he would do *anything* someone asks him! Even if it's really wrong!"

"You might be right, Libby," Caleb said. "He sure doesn't look like someone I'd like to meet in a dark alley."

"Why did Jordan run away?" the fiddler asked.

Caleb didn't answer at once, as if wondering how much to tell. Finally he said, "We don't trust the pawnbroker."

"Because Jordan is a fugitive?" Franz asked.

Caleb was in a spot now. Libby knew he wouldn't lie, yet what could he say? Even on free soil such as Minnesota Territory, slave catchers had the legal right to gather a group of men, arrest a runaway, and bring him back to his owner.

The fiddler studied Caleb's face. "You are afraid to tell me? Don't you think I know that Jordan is a runaway slave?"

Franz looked from Caleb to Jordan to Libby. "We don't have your kind of slaves in my country. But we have another kind of person held in bondage. I will protect Jordan the way he protected me on the *Christina*."

Your country, Libby wondered. *Where is it?*

Before she could ask, Jordan drew a deep breath of relief and offered his thanks. Caleb said more. "Is there any other way we can help you?"

As though a mask had slipped down over his face, the fiddler shook his head. "If you find my violin, it is gut. I will be grateful forever."

He's afraid again, Libby thought. *He's trying to say we can trust him. At the same time, he doesn't trust us. I wonder why?*

Libby felt sure it had something to do with Shadowman. Since the concert, Libby had kept on looking for the man in the long black coat. Because his hat shadowed his face, Libby wondered if she would ever recognize him.

Soon after they returned to the *Christina*, Annika found Libby. "Would you like to go with me to find Harriet?" she asked. Known as St. Paul's first schoolteacher, Harriet Bishop was also Annika's friend.

"Did you find out where Miss Bishop lives?" Libby asked as they crossed the riverfront.

"No, but everyone knows her. We won't have any trouble."

As it turned out, the search proved more difficult than either Libby or Annika expected. While it was easy to get directions, it was difficult to follow them. Directly up from the Lower Landing was Jackson Street, and a creek ran alongside it.

After backtracking to the bridge over the creek, they discovered streets that twisted around until both of them felt confused. Whenever she came to an open view, Annika looked toward the river to be sure they headed in the right direction. Often the construction work on streets forced them to make long trips around. As the August sun beat down upon them, Libby grew more and more tired.

"They must have had a good rain before we came," Annika

said finally. Holding up her skirt, she walked around another mud hole.

After coming up the Mississippi in low water, neither of them wanted to complain about rain. But even Annika seemed overwhelmed by the mud. "There's a tree with a bit of grass under it. Let's sit down and rest."

The shade was welcome to both of them, and soon Annika asked, "Libby, what was your mother like?"

Libby smiled. "Kind. Fun. You know how Pa asked us to think about what we want most? What we care about? Ma wanted to help people. Auntie wants things. That's one of the reasons Pa had me come back to live with him."

Now Libby felt grateful for that hurtful night in Burlington, Iowa, when Pa made up his mind. "At first after Ma died, Pa knew I was too young to live on the boat without a mother. Then he knew he had no choice but to have me with him."

"What happened?" Annika asked.

Libby hesitated. She had changed so much in five months that she didn't like telling Annika what she had been like. But maybe Annika needed to know. "I was turning into a spoiled brat."

"Hmmm." Annika had that look of mischief again. "I wonder how that came about. But I guess you aren't a spoiled child anymore."

"I guess," Libby said. But sometimes she wasn't real sure.

When they found Miss Bishop, she invited them in for afternoon tea. "Annika! In all my life, I never expected to see you here!"

Annika's warm laugh showed her delight in surprising her friend. "When you encouraged me to become a teacher, you didn't have any idea that I'd follow you?"

Twenty-six-year-old Annika was fourteen years younger, but Miss Bishop had talked to her about teaching when Annika was a child. She had never forgotten it.

Libby knew the teacher had come to St. Paul as a Baptist missionary. Her dark hair waved softly around her face, falling in tight, long curls to her shoulders. Her clear eyes gave Libby the feeling that the teacher usually knew where she was going and how to get there.

"What was it like when you first came?" Libby asked.

"There was no bookstore within three hundred miles. My school was a ten- by twenty-foot log house with a bark roof. It had three windows and a door so low I had to stoop to go in. At one time the building was used as a stable."

Miss Bishop's eyes filled with laughter. "A friendly chicken wandered in and out. The nine children in my class spoke three different languages. But I could not have been happier if I were a queen. I felt I would not trade what I was doing with any person who lived."

Miss Bishop offered Libby and Annika lemonade and cookies, then sat down. "We've come a long way since then. In a couple of weeks we'll dedicate the first school building built by the city with public funds. It's even built of stone."

"And now you have an island named after you!" Annika said. "You've also written a book. Congratulations!"

After a time Miss Bishop leaned forward, saying, "Annika, it's good to just talk. But what can I do for you?"

"I'd like to teach in the area. Do you know of an opening?"

"You just came up the river?"

Annika nodded.

"You're sure you can handle our long, cold winters? Being cut off from the rest of the world?"

"I don't know," Annika said honestly. "I've never lived in the kind of winters everyone describes. Just walking your streets is difficult."

"Ah yes, our streets." Miss Bishop smiled and offered Libby another cookie. "They also get very filled with snow. And it can be lonely here."

"But you survived," Annika said.

"With the Lord's help. When it was really difficult, I remembered how He led me here. Is God asking you to come?"

Annika nodded. "I believe He wants me in St. Paul this winter."

"Then I'll see if there's an opening somewhere. Can you come back tomorrow?"

When she said good-bye to Miss Bishop, Annika's eyes shone, but Libby felt afraid for her. With each step through the muddy streets, Libby's worry grew. Finally her words spilled over. "Please, Annika, won't you come with us instead?"

The teacher shook her head.

"We'll go south where it's warmer," Libby promised. "People say that in St. Paul it gets so cold you can freeze your nose."

Annika laughed. "I'll watch out for that."

"I'll worry about you this winter."

"No, you won't." Annika circled a low spot in the street. "You'll be just fine without me."

Libby offered the smile she had practiced on the boys in Chicago. "Pa would like to have you come with us."

A grim schoolteacher's look entered Annika's face, but Libby hurried on. "If you married Pa, life would be much easier for you."

One step away from a mud puddle, Annika stopped. "Libby, isn't your father able to speak for himself?"

"Oh yes!" Libby exclaimed. She opened her mouth, trying to make things better, but no words came.

In the next instant Annika stepped into the puddle. It was deep—so deep that muddy water splashed up, covering Annika's dress as high as her knees. Just in time she caught herself from falling.

"Oh, Annika!" Libby moaned as she helped the teacher to drier ground. Libby wanted to hide her head in shame. "I'm sorry! It's all my fault!"

Annika sighed. "Yes, Libby, it is. But I forgive you. Let's forget about it, all right?"

Libby nodded, but now something else bothered her. "There's mud on your cheek."

Taking out her handkerchief, Annika scrubbed her face. As they started walking again, she said, "Libby, there's something I'm wondering about. If I married your pa, how do you think you and I would get along?"

"You'd be my friend," Libby answered quickly.

"Sometimes I would be your friend—someone to talk with. But I would also be your mother."

Gone was the mischief Libby often saw in Annika's eyes. "I would not replace your mother, Christina. No one could do that.

No one *should* do that. But there would be times when I'd have to *act* like a mother."

"You mean get after me?"

"Correct you," Annika said. "I would need to tell you what you're doing wrong so you'd learn to change. Are you ready for that?"

Libby found it hard to believe there would be such a time. She and Annika were friends. Libby was sure that would continue forever. "You don't need to worry. I'll behave."

But Annika only smiled.

They walked the rest of the way in silence. To add to Annika's embarrassment, Pa was standing on the main deck when she and Libby hurried up the gangplank. As always Pa looked tall and handsome in his captain's uniform. He also looked clean.

Annika tried to slip around him, but Pa stopped her. "You've discovered the St. Paul streets."

Clearly embarrassed, Annika nodded.

"I'm sorry," Pa said.

"So am I." Then Annika laughed. "Well, it's just my pride that's hurt. I'm glad I found the mud *after* talking to Harriet Bishop, not before."

"You were looking for work?" Pa asked quickly. "I wanted to talk with you again about teaching on the *Christina*."

"Never mind," Annika said. "Libby already has."

Pa's look told Libby all she needed to know. Her father did not appreciate her help. Suddenly Libby felt as if she were the one with mud on her dress.

"Miss Berg," Pa said. "It would be my pleasure if I could take you to see the less muddy sights of St. Paul. We could even have dinner at a fine hotel."

Annika smiled. "Thank you, Captain Norstad. I would like that very much. I'll be ready as soon as I find some good, clean water."

Libby soon learned that Franz had heard about a St. Paul music store that also sold toys. While Jordan stayed behind to find a way to St. Anthony, Caleb, Libby, and Franz set out. As they walked through the streets, he told them about his wife and daughter.

When she stepped inside the music store, Libby saw all kinds of wonderful things hanging on the wall. A large brass instrument, a cello, a pendulum clock, and a china doll. On a counter nearby was a small merry-go-round with carved wooden horses.

From her years in Chicago, Libby felt sure that many of the toys were imported from England, France, and Germany. In spite of the condition of its streets, St. Paul had grown far beyond being a frontier town. *No wonder Auntie enjoys shopping here!*

Now Franz explained about the theft. The shopkeeper felt sure he had seen the violin that morning.

"A good violin is like a painting," he said. "It has an autograph, a signature of its own."

"If we found your violin, how would we know it was yours?" Libby asked Franz.

"I'll show you," the shopkeeper answered. From the wall he took down a violin and turned it over. "This one is made of choice wood." Lightly he passed his hand over the back of the instrument. "See the grain in the wood? The beautiful pattern? But the wood of *his* violin is unequaled for beauty."

"How can I describe it?" Franz shrugged his shoulders. "The back is smooth and flowing—like a river, it is. Yes, that is it."

Franz turned back to the shopkeeper. "And the sound?" he asked, as if wanting to make sure there was no doubt. "You played the violin?"

"The highest quality. Better than any of my own good instruments. The best of any violin I have played. I couldn't give the man the amount of money he asked. I offered him everything in my store, but he wanted gold, not trade."

"What about the violin?" Libby asked, hardly breathing. "Where is it now?"

"I'm sorry," the shopkeeper told Franz. "I had no idea the man was a thief, but even so, it pained me to send him on. I told him about a man who came in with the Red River oxcarts. You can find him at Larpenteur's Lake. He has saved his gold for many years, and he just sold his furs for this season. I knew he might have the amount of gold needed."

"The thief who brought the violin here. Can you describe him?" Caleb asked.

"Tall. Brown hair. Blue eyes."

Libby and Caleb looked at each other. Tall, brown hair, blue eyes? Countless men might fill that description.

"Brown hair, not blond?" Libby asked.

"That's right."

Did the pawnbroker lie to us? Libby wondered. His description fit half the Swedes in Minnesota.

"Did the man have a beard or mustache?" Libby asked.

The shopkeeper shook his head. "But he had a red mark on his neck, just below the jawline on the left side."

"So!" Franz exclaimed. "The thief plays the violin?"

"Yes, he plainly had an area of roughened skin from the chin rest of the violin."

The shopkeeper held out his own violin to Franz. "Please," he said. "Do me the honor of playing on my humble instrument."

Franz took the violin and stepped away from Libby and Caleb to where there was more room. Standing behind the counter, he faced them and the door. When the shopkeeper sat down to listen, Franz raised the bow.

From the first notes, Libby knew he was playing the Hungarian Rhapsody she had heard on the *Christina*. As the music rose like the soaring of eagles, Franz closed his eyes and seemed to dream of a country far away.

Just then Libby felt Caleb's hand on her shoulder. For an instant he tightened his fingers as though warning her. Then Libby heard the sound.

A man had entered the shop. A man who walked quietly over to where the shopkeeper sat. Libby turned just slightly and felt glad for Caleb's warning.

Feeling that she had drawn his picture only moments before, Libby recognized the man. As she saw the cruel lines around his mouth, a shiver went down her spine.

In the next moment Mr. Trouble looked directly at Libby. His eyes widened with surprise, and Libby knew that he recognized her.

"Good afternoon, Miss Norstad," he said. His words were polite, but the coldness in his face cut through to her heart.

As if he wished to buy something, Mr. Trouble walked over to a counter. Watching him, Libby started shaking.

10

Thieves!

As Libby edged closer to Caleb, she saw the fiddler's eyes. No longer lost in his music, he watched the man's every movement.

When the shopkeeper asked, "May I help you with something?" Mr. Trouble shook his head and headed for the door. His hand on the knob, he turned back to stare at Libby once more.

The moment Mr. Trouble left the shop, Libby leaned over the counter. As she covered her face, her hands trembled. Through her fear came one thought. *Why does he want the picture I drew of him?*

Franz stopped playing. "What's wrong?"

But Caleb spoke to Libby instead. "You're okay, he's gone." Caleb spoke softly, and Libby knew he was trying to comfort her. "Stay here with Franz. I want to see where Mr. Trouble goes."

"Who was that man?" Franz asked when Caleb hurried out.

With an effort Libby pulled herself together. "Suspect number two. Mr. Trouble. Tall. Brown hair. Blue eyes. Do you know him?"

Franz shook his head. He turned to the shopkeeper. "Is he the man who offered you the violin?"

"I've never seen him before. But there *is* something I want to offer you. Do you need a place to stay?"

Franz looked at Libby. "When the *Christina* leaves St. Paul, yes, I do. But without a violin, I have no way to earn my living."

"While you search for your violin, I'll loan you my best one. I'll introduce you to men and women who can give you work. The people of St. Paul will be honored to have you live among us."

When Caleb returned, Mr. Trouble had given him the slip. "Even if I found out where he's staying, we can't prove anything," Caleb said.

On their way back to the Lower Landing, Libby and Caleb talked with Franz about it.

"There were three men on the *Christina* who could have taken your violin," Libby said. "The man who works in the pawnshop is short. Two other men are tall. You just saw one of them—Mr. Trouble, who got upset when I drew his picture. The other man stood in the shadows during your concert. Did you recognize him?"

"His face? I could not see it."

"Is there anyone who might want to get even with you?" Caleb asked.

The fiddler drew back. "Here in America?" As Franz shook his head, the mask went down over his face.

After Franz left them, Libby and Caleb took Samson for a walk along the riverfront. There they could talk without anyone hearing them.

"The fiddler is hiding something," Libby said.

"You're sure?" Caleb asked. "I feel I can trust Franz."

"I trust him too. But there's something he doesn't want us to know." Libby paused, trying to think how to explain. "It's like there's something really important in his life that he's afraid to talk about."

Caleb stared at her. "I think you're on to something. What could it be?"

"To start with, he's a famous violinist. He doesn't tell us, but that isn't hard to guess."

"He probably plays with a well-known symphony," Caleb said. "But if that's true, why doesn't he tell us?"

"Maybe he's humble."

Caleb disagreed. "You can be humble but still tell people what your work is. You just don't brag about it. I think it's something more."

"Let's think what we know about him," Libby said. "We already know he has a young son. Today he talked about a wife and daughter. He's come to America—"

"That's it!" Caleb exclaimed. "He's come here to America, but why? *Why* did he come here? And why doesn't he have his family along? That's where he always stops talking."

"And he never talks about what country or city he's from. Maybe he's running away from an argument with his family."

Caleb shook his head. "Franz isn't the kind that holds a grudge. He's too soft down inside. He says what he thinks, but if he had an argument, I think he'd work it out."

Libby agreed with Caleb. "But what could his secret be? He wears tattered clothes as if he's poor."

Caleb pounced on that. "*As if he's poor*. Do you think he is?"

Libby shook her head. "Not really poor. Not like people who have no food to eat. I think he had a lot of money once, but now, for some reason, it's gone. Do you suppose Kadosa is his real name?"

"You know, I wondered the same thing. If we question even that, what could his secret be?"

Libby didn't like the feeling it gave her. "Lots of immigrants change their names when they come to America. Yohansson to Johnson, for instance."

"I'm not talking about that," Caleb said, "and neither are you."

When Pa returned from taking Annika out for dinner, he whistled coming up the stairs. As he rocked back and forth in his big chair, Libby sat on the low stool beside him. It was Libby's favorite time of the day—the moments when she and Pa talked together.

"You know, Libby, there's something I've been thinking about for quite a while. Someday the railroads will replace us—"

"Replace steamboats?" The idea startled Libby.

"More and more railroad lines are reaching the banks of the Mississippi. Right now they bring us business. But the time will come when railroads stretch from sea to sea. When the iron horse replaces steamboats, I'll need another way of life."

The idea of such a thing happening was so new to Libby that she couldn't even imagine Pa being anything else. But her father went on.

"After all that happened earlier this summer, I've had a good season. I've paid off my crew, and there's money left over. Now, while I have it, I want to invest that money in land."

"As speculation?" Knowing Pa, Libby found that hard to believe.

"As a way of planning ahead. A way of working toward a secret dream. I want to take a look around and see if I can find land on a river bluff. Though I might need to leave steamboats, the river will never leave me. If that time comes, I want trees and hills and a view of the river. Enough land to cut wood and grow crops and live—"

"And have a family?" Libby asked.

Reaching out, Pa drew Libby close in a hug. "We are a family. A never-give-up family. Remember?"

"A family that doesn't give up on each other, even when things are hard." Remembering Annika's reaction to her matchmaking, Libby felt afraid to say more. Then she took a risk. "*More* of a family, I mean."

"Yes. More people in our family." A smile lurked in Pa's eyes. "Let's start by seeing what Annika thinks about your idea. Would you like that?"

"If you mean marrying Annika, I would like that," Libby said. "But I think you need to convince her."

As Pa sighed, the smile in his eyes disappeared. "She needs convincing, all right. She's a mighty independent young woman. I think a part of Annika is running scared."

"I think so too," Libby said, but deep down she had a very big wish. *I hope Pa never finds out I told Annika to marry him.*

Glad that Mr. Trouble was off the *Christina*, Libby took her blankets back to her room and made her bed there. If Mr. Trouble was the one who looked through her belongings, he was gone now. Out of her life. Or so Libby believed.

That night Libby went to bed with a singing heart. Long after everyone else on the *Christina* was quiet, she still felt excited about Pa and Annika. Just thinking about them, Libby turned around and around on her corn-husk mattress.

When she heard Pa going down the stairs to see if all was well, Libby decided that sleep wasn't going to come. Getting up, she dressed quickly and went out to sit on the hurricane deck. From her favorite place, she had a good view of the nearby warehouses, the bluff along the river, and the city of St. Paul.

Soon Libby pulled on a sweater. The cool night after a warm day reminded her that this was Minnesota Territory. Before long autumn would come, then the real cold. *Maybe Annika will be with us, and we'll be far away.*

The riverfront was quiet now. The moon rode high, covered by a line of clouds. Above Libby, the line of warehouses stood out, a deeper black than the night sky.

For a long time Libby sat there. Then, as she started to stand up and return to her room, she heard a sound. What was it? Muffled footsteps? The creak of a harness?

In the street at one end of the warehouses, Libby sensed a movement. Leaning forward, she peered into the darkness.

Then she saw it: a horse-drawn wagon backing onto the narrow ledge of land this side of the warehouse. The wagon stopped next to the back door. Soon another wagon joined the first. Then a third wagon crowded into the narrow space.

A man climbed down from each wagon. Two were tall and one was short. All three quietly slipped in through the door.

Why? Libby wondered. *What are they doing?*

A moment later they began coming back out. Each man carried something heavy on his shoulder. As the moon broke free of the clouds, Libby saw what it was. A pack of furs!

Thieves! Libby thought as she watched them load the wagons. *Thieves stealing the furs!*

Just then Libby heard the *Christina*'s gangplank go out and quiet footsteps pass over to the riverbank. In the dark area near the boat, two men started toward the wagons.

More thieves! What can I do?

As Libby stood up to tell her pa, she remembered he wasn't in his cabin. By the time she found him, the thieves would get away.

Then Libby caught sight of the nearby bell. In one moment she was there, taking hold of the long rope between the bell and pilothouse.

11

Riggs!

With one tug of the rope, the bell rang out. The clanging sound filled the night, and the Lower Landing came alive. Again and again Libby rang the bell.

On the *Christina* deckhands raced up the stairs to see what was wrong. Near the warehouse the thieves leaped into their wagons. As men from the *Christina* raced toward them, Libby stood at the railing, watching. Just then two policemen rounded one end of the building.

At the other end of the warehouse, the thieves cracked whips over their horses. Rattling and swaying, the wagons entered the street. The policemen tore after them, but the thieves got away.

When all the excitement was over, Libby walked slowly to her father's cabin. Filled with discouragement, she waited for Pa to come in. *I tried*, she thought. *But it wasn't enough.*

It was Caleb who came first, and he asked, "Libby, how do you manage to get in so much trouble?"

Libby stared at him. "Caleb Whitney, I was trying to stop the thieves. I wanted to warn the police, the people who owned the warehouse, anyone who would listen."

"You warned people, all right. You got everyone on the whole waterfront awake. But the thieves got away before Jordan and I could see who they were."

"That was *you* along the riverfront? Well, I'll tell you who they were. Two were tall, and one was short enough to be the pawnbroker."

Caleb barely listened. Instead he asked, "Couldn't you think of another way to get help?"

Libby bowed her head. Closing her fists, she gripped them until her fingernails bit into the palms of her hands. Not for anything in the world would she let Caleb see her cry.

But he wasn't finished yet. "Libby, you made yourself a marked person again. Those thieves know who you are. They know there's only one captain's daughter on the *Christina*."

Like water, a flood of anger poured through Libby. But when she looked up, she saw Caleb's eyes. "You're scared, aren't you?" she said.

"How can I *not* be scared? From the minute you came to live on this boat, your pa asked me to look out for you."

"So-o-o-o," Libby said. "I'm part of your job."

Caleb groaned. "No! I mean yes! Oh, you know what I mean."

"No, I don't." Libby's anger was back, and this time it spilled over. "I thought we were friends. I thought you liked having me help with the Underground Railroad, that you trusted me—"

Suddenly Caleb whirled around and stalked off. At the door he turned back. "Libby, you make me so mad I could spit!"

Then he was gone.

As the door slammed behind him, Libby giggled. *So! Even the great Caleb Whitney can get upset!*

Then her giggling gave way to sobs. Half a minute later, she remembered Caleb's scared eyes and started laughing. But when she once more started weeping, she sobbed as if she would never stop.

Just then Caleb flung open the door and pushed Samson inside. "Keep him with you," he warned. "I can't be your nursemaid all the time."

"I don't want you to be my nursemaid *any* of the time!" Libby called after him. But Caleb was gone for good.

❖

In Pa's cabin the next morning, Libby finished telling him what had happened during the night. Cup of coffee in hand and still taking it easy, Pa looked through the window to Jackson Street. "There's Joe Rolette!"

With quick strides a man was hurrying down the steep bluff, headed straight for the *Christina*.

"Who's Joe Rolette?" Libby asked.

"The representative from Pembina—by the Canadian border where the oxcarts come from. Because of men like Joe and his partner, St. Paul takes an active part in international trade."

Already Pa was looking for his tie. "Joe is also the man who stole the bill that would have moved the capital of Minnesota from St. Paul to St. Peter. He walked off with the bill and hid out in a St. Paul hotel till it was too late to take a vote."

Libby giggled. No doubt the people of Minnesota Territory took it seriously, though.

"Joe uses sled dogs to come to St. Paul in winter. Libby, where's my toothbrush?"

"It's not on your washstand?"

"And my comb? That's not here either."

Libby hurried over to look. Pa was so orderly she had never seen him search for his belongings.

As he laid out his captain's coat, he said, "My clothes brush. And where are my shoes?"

Upset now, Pa looked around. "What's going on? Everything I need has disappeared!"

"Uh-oh!" Libby said. "Did Peter offer to help you yesterday?"

Suddenly Pa stood still. "Why, yes, now that I think of it. When he asked what he could do, I suggested he straighten my cabin."

Instead of its usual place on the washstand, Libby found Pa's toothbrush in his desk. His comb had somehow fallen down between the bed and the wall. His clothes brush and shoes were in a drawer under the bed.

By the time Pa put on his captain's coat and hat, he looked exhausted. And Joe Rolette was knocking at the door.

"Can you manage to find some other way for Peter to help?" Pa asked as Libby scurried out.

At breakfast Pa told Annika, "I'm going to take a look around today. Would you like to come with me?"

"I'd like to go," Annika said, "but I promised to check back with Harriet. She's looking for a teaching position for me."

Pa looked disappointed. "I'd still like to have you help me teach on the *Christina* if you're willing. You could also teach English to immigrants as they travel upstream."

Before Annika could answer, Peter jumped in to ask Pa, "How can I help you today? Shall I clean your cabin again?"

Taking Peter's slate, Pa wrote quickly, "I'd like your help in another way. If you want to be an explorer, how about going with me?"

While rousters loaded Joe Rolette's furs onto the *Christina*, Pa set out with Peter. From the boat Libby watched them cross the waterfront.

"Peter gets to be with Pa for a whole day," she told Annika.

"Libby, Peter needs a sister just like you," Annika said gently. "And he needs your pa in the same way that you need him. Your father has enough love for both of you."

But Libby's gaze followed Pa long after he and Peter started up Jackson Street. *I've always had Pa to myself. My life is changing. I don't know if I like the changes.*

On the riverfront Libby and Franz watched Jordan and Caleb go from one wagon to the next. Before long they found a farmer headed for the young city of St. Anthony. On his way there, he would pass near Larpenteur's Lake, where the oxcart drivers camped.

Franz swung up to the high seat next to the driver while Libby, Caleb, and Jordan climbed in at the back. As they bumped along, Jordan leaned against the high boards at the front of the wagon. His eyes closed, he hummed so softly that Libby could barely hear him.

When Jordan began singing the words, Franz turned his head to listen. Swaying back and forth with the music, Jordan seemed to forget where he was.

"Deep River, my home is over Jordan;
Deep River; Lord, I want to cross over into camp ground;
Lord, I want to cross over into camp ground."

As though there had been no months between, Libby remembered the first time she heard Jordan sing. His back raw and bleeding, he sat in the sun while Caleb washed his wounds.

"Don't you hate your owner Riggs?" Libby had asked when she learned about the beating.

"I wants to be angry—to hate him with all my soul," Jordan told her. *"But hatin' robs your bones of strength, makes you blind when you needs to fight. If you forgive, you be strong."*

From that moment on, Libby's life had been forever changed by what she saw in Jordan and his family. For them, crossing a river meant escaping from slavery into a new life of freedom. But it also meant something more. The strong spiritual life that Jordan and his family shared was like a flowing river.

"Oh, don't you want to go to that gospel feast,
That promised land where all is peace?"

Like a cry the words came from deep within. Softly Franz began to hum along. Jordan's voice grew stronger and stronger.

"Lord, I want to cross over into camp ground;
Lord, I want to cross over into camp ground."

When the farmer stopped at the trail to Larpenteur's Lake, Jordan stayed in the wagon as it went on to St. Anthony. Libby, Caleb, and Franz walked the rest of the way to the camp of the oxcart drivers.

From Pa Libby had learned that the drivers were of French, Scotch, English, Cree, and Ojibwa ancestry. Each of their carts carried about a thousand pounds of furs from Manitoba and the Red River Valley. Usually the drivers started south in June, and the long walk took about forty days. More than once Pa had wondered why they had arrived so late in the season.

Soon Libby heard the light, quick tunes of a fiddle. As Franz started walking faster, she asked, "Do you think that's your violin?"

They found the campsite on the shores of a small lake. Here and there was a covered wagon, but some of the drivers had set up tepees. Others had thrown buffalo hides over their carts to make tents. Nearby, oxen and mules grazed on the prairie grass.

A few men sat on logs around a campfire and wore blue shirts with metal buttons and red sashes around their waists. Often their faces were dark and lined from being in the wind and sun. Two of the men were shaping new axles for their carts. Other men repaired harnesses for their return trip to the far north.

Among the drivers were a handful of women and children. The women's carts were brightly painted, and they had washed crusted mud from the spokes and rim.

When Libby asked about their carts, a woman explained. "If we cross a river, we take off the wheels and tie four of them together to make a raft."

The wheels were bowed, and the drivers used a lining of buffalo hides to protect the furs from water. Now the carts no longer held furs, but some were partly filled with supplies for the trip home and the winter ahead.

The woman also told Libby why they were late in reaching St. Paul. There had been much sickness. Often axles on the carts broke and needed to be replaced. More than once oxen had stumbled into bogs. What appeared to be solid ground shook for ten or fifteen feet around.

At the campfire the oxcart driver played one lively tune after another. When he stopped, Franz motioned to the fiddle and asked, "May I?"

The driver sized Franz up.

"I'll be careful," he promised at once. "I'm a fiddler too."

With the bow dancing across the strings, Franz played the melody the driver had just finished. When Franz stopped, he turned the fiddle over. As though liking the feel of the wood, he gently rubbed the back side.

Carefully Franz handed the fiddle back to its owner. "Do I have the tune right?"

The other man beamed. "Just about. You have a good ear. I'll show you the place you're missing." Using short, quick bows, the driver played one part of the tune again.

Tapping his toe and nodding his head in time to the music, Franz hummed along with the fiddle. Finally he said, "Thank you, thank you! Now I have it! Whenever I play your song, I'll think of you."

"And I you!" As the driver bowed low, his red sash touched the ground. "When I tell my children of this moment, I will say a great man played my fiddle."

Leaving the camp behind, Libby, Caleb, and Franz started back to the trail that led to St. Anthony and St. Paul.

"Was it your violin?" Libby asked.

Franz shook his head. "But a gut one it is. Did you hear how sweetly she sang? The man not only has a gut fiddle. He is an excellent fiddler. That is why he saved his gold for an even better violin."

Now Franz looked disappointed. "So close we came to finding my violin. The driver thought the thief didn't really want to sell it. Much, much gold he wanted. No one could buy it."

"Do you collect songs wherever you go?" Libby asked. "Is that how you learned to play different kinds of music?"

Franz smiled. "I was a child when my nurse took me on visits to her village. I danced to the tunes of country fiddlers. Their music entered my blood, and I never forgot it."

Soon they reached the trail where stagecoaches ran twice a day between St. Paul and St. Anthony. The stage heading back to St. Paul came first, and Franz swung aboard. Before long another stage stopped to take Libby and Caleb to St. Anthony.

"We have another clue," Libby said as the horses moved out.

"I know," Caleb answered. "If Franz had a nurse take care of him when he was a boy, he came from a well-to-do family."

"I've been thinking about something else." Libby remembered the day the fiddler didn't answer when she called him Mr. Kadosa. "I think Franz is his real first name. That's why he asked us to use it."

Soon the stagecoach brought them to the east side of the Mississippi River. Looking ahead, Libby saw the five-story brick building called the Winslow House. A high flight of steps led up to the main entrance of the hotel.

Near that entrance Libby noticed a swift blur of color. Someone ran down the steps, across the road, then down more steps to the riverbank. Libby leaned forward to see. Could that possibly be Jordan? He was too far away to be sure.

As the stage drew closer, Libby saw a well-dressed man standing at the top of the hotel steps. In his hand was a gold-headed cane. Forgotten now was the blur of someone running—the person Libby could barely see. The man on the steps held her full attention.

"I have a terrible feeling," she whispered. "Do you think Mr. Thompson understood that Jordan is a fugitive?"

Caleb knew exactly what she was saying. "He probably thought Jordan was a free black like himself. That Jordan has freedom papers, and it's safe to send him here. He might be in big trouble."

When the stage came to a stop, Libby's guess turned into a nightmare. The tightness in her stomach changed to a fear she couldn't push aside.

"Caleb," Libby said, barely able to speak. "Look who's standing on the steps."

Caleb glanced that way, then jerked to attention. "Is that really Riggs?" Not only was the man Jordan's owner and most dreaded enemy. He was a cruel slavetrader as well.

Caleb balled his fists in anger. "Of all the places in the world where Riggs might be! How could Jordan possibly come to the same hotel?"

12

Dreaded Friend

"*Riggs* must be here to escape the heat." Libby's voice was small.

"Well, I guess it's not such a big surprise," Caleb answered. "Your pa said that of all the hotels in the area, this is the one people from the South like best. It has every luxury a hotel can offer and a view of the falls besides."

Just then the stagecoach driver climbed down from his high seat. Opening the door, he called, "Everybody out!" But Libby could not move.

When the driver tried to hurry them along, Caleb said, "We've decided to go a bit farther."

"Can't go any farther. End of the line."

Caleb glanced around. Riggs still stood on the top step at the main hotel entrance. It wasn't hard to see that he was searching for someone.

"We can't get out," Libby whispered. "That must have been Jordan running away. If Riggs sees us, he'll have no doubt that Jordan is here."

"We'll wait in the stagecoach," Caleb told the driver. "We'll ride with you back to St. Paul."

"That's at least an hour from now," the driver said. He tipped his head toward the hotel. "You'll have to wait inside."

Instead, Caleb stood up, grasped the handle on the far side of the stagecoach, and opened the door. When he stepped down, Libby followed him. The stagecoach stood between them and the man on the steps.

"Keep your back to Riggs," Caleb whispered to Libby. "Pretend you're enjoying a walk."

Caleb crooked his arm, and Libby took it. From his high seat on the coach, the driver called to his horses, "Giddyup!"

But Libby had no time to enjoy her first view of the beautiful falls. Instead, she prickled with nervousness. It took all her willpower to not look around to see if Riggs was still on the steps, watching.

Without turning his head even to talk with Libby, Caleb kept his back to the Winslow House. Just as Libby felt she could no longer bear the suspense, they reached the river.

Ahead lay two islands, with Hennepin on their left and the larger Nicollet Island off to their right. Sloping sharply downward, the riverbank looked muddy, as if from recent rains.

"It's going to be slippery," Caleb said. "Hang on to my arm and don't make a scene. When we're halfway down, Riggs won't be able to see us."

Libby felt sure that the minute she stepped onto the miry bank she would sink in. When she drew back, Caleb tugged her arm and moved ahead.

It was every bit as bad as Libby expected. As they walked down the bank into the lower land next to the river, Libby slipped, but Caleb hung on. The next instant her right foot sank deep in the soft ground.

Libby stopped, afraid. "Are there snakes here?"

"Probably. Keep moving." Caleb tugged on her arm. "We aren't out of sight yet."

As Libby stepped forward, her left foot also sank deep. Within two more steps, mud rose to her ankles, almost oozing into her high-top shoes.

Libby gasped. "Oh, Caleb, I can't stand it!"

"You have to!" Caleb's voice did not allow her to disagree. "If Riggs catches Jordan, it's his life. Keep going no matter what!"

Struggling to pull out her feet, but sinking again at each step, Libby wailed, "But *where* are we going?"

"First, out of sight. Second, to find Jordan. He must have seen Riggs and that's what sent him running."

"You think Jordan is here?"

"Where else can he be? Somehow we have to get him to a place where he's safe."

Ahead of Libby lay the edge of the river. Keeping her gaze on the rocks, she moved on. Soon the pounding rush of the waterfalls drowned out even Caleb's shouted words.

Caught by the swiftly moving current, huge logs rode free, tumbling over the falls to the calmer water below. Caleb turned upstream, following the edge of the river.

Before long they reached a large sawmill. Great piles of logs filled the land along the river. Nearby stood a smaller gristmill. Outside, horses stood harnessed to farm wagons while their owners waited for their grain to be ground.

Only when they stepped behind a pile of logs did Caleb stop. Peering around one end, he looked back. Libby turned with him.

At least two blocks behind them, the Winslow House rose higher than the surrounding buildings. Caleb was right. If Riggs was still standing on the front steps, he was out of sight.

As Caleb faced upstream again, he dropped Libby's arm. Caleb moved ahead quickly now, thinking only about finding Jordan.

Across the river on the west bank was another sawmill and gristmill. Still an infant village, Minneapolis was no match for the sprawling village of St. Anthony, which lay along the east bank of the falls. With its many frame houses built from lumber sawed in the mills, St. Anthony looked like views Libby had seen of small New England cities.

By now the panic in her stomach had settled into a tight, hard knot. "If Jordan is here, where can he be?"

Caleb shook his head. "Most anywhere. St. Anthony has over four thousand people!"

"If only we had some way to know which direction Jordan went," Libby answered. "Peter gave us a secret sign. Do you think Jordan would remember?"

They began by searching for his boot prints, but the muddy land was filled with countless tracks. Then, near a bridge to Nicollet Island, Libby saw what she hoped for.

"Look!" She pointed down. "Peter's fish! And the head of the fish points toward the island!"

After crossing the bridge to the island, they checked the ground again. This time a fish pointed off to the right. As with the first fish, it had been drawn in a hurry.

From one secret sign to the next, Libby and Caleb followed Jordan. Sometimes the fish were easy to find. Other times they were half hidden, as if drawn while Jordan knelt beneath a bush. His trail headed up the island past a house, then looped around, coming back to a wooded area close to the falls.

When at last they caught up with Jordan, he had found refuge in a clump of trees. Watered by the spray of the rapids, the leaves were so thick that they hid Jordan completely. Without the sign of the fish, they might have missed him.

As Jordan looked up and saw them, he trembled. "If Riggs can find me here—here in Minnesota Territory—where can I be free?" Gone was all the confidence with which Jordan usually acted.

"You'll be okay," Caleb told him.

For Jordan, who had grown used to hiding from slave catchers, there was something much bigger. "But my family sent me here to spy out the land. Where can they be safe?"

"We'll figure it out," Caleb said, trying to encourage him.

They decided to try for help at one of the mills. Walking back, Caleb found a farmer who planned to drive across the prairie to St. Paul.

Soon after Caleb returned, the farmer drove close to the Nicollet Island bridge and stopped his horses. When Jordan started to stand up, Caleb said, "Wait for the signal. He'll get water."

Libby was curious. "How did you know who to ask?"

"I prayed," Caleb told her. "Then I started asking questions. This man took me aside, as if he guessed what I needed."

The sun had passed its highest point when the farmer picked up a bucket from the back of the wagon. At the river he filled it with water.

"That means there's no one watching," Caleb told Jordan as the farmer started watering his horses. "When you get to his wagon, there will be two burlap bags. Crawl into one of them and pull the other over your head."

Following Jordan, Libby and Caleb sat with him in the back of the wagon. Surrounded by the high board sides, they rode to St. Paul.

"Did Riggs see you?" Libby asked Jordan when he pushed the burlap bag away from his face.

"I don't know," he answered. "I took one look at him and took off like a bolt of lightning."

The moment they reached the *Christina*, Jordan headed up the stairs to the top deck. With slumped shoulders and bowed head, he leaned back against the wall of the texas. He looked as discouraged as Libby had ever seen him.

When Peter joined them, Caleb used the slate to explain all that had happened. "Jordan used your secret sign to help us find him!"

"He did?" Peter was delighted. Then he saw Jordan's face. Reaching out, Peter put his hand on his shoulder and asked, "Why are you afraid?"

Jordan tipped back his head and opened his eyes. Without turning his head, he glanced sideways at Peter with a look that asked, "What did you say?"

Peter repeated his question. "Why are you afraid?"

For a few minutes Jordan sat there, still without speaking. Then he slapped his knee and laughed.

"I forgot!" Again Jordan laughed as though the biggest joke was on him.

Peter looked puzzled, but Caleb kept writing.

"When I was a slave," Jordan said, "I dreamed about being free. I dreamed about bringing my family to freedom. Now that I'm free, I have to do what Mr. Thompson said."

Jordan clapped the ten-year-old on the back. "Thanks, Peter. You just reminded me that I have to live freedom!"

A few minutes later Libby found Pa in his cabin. He was eager to talk about the land he found. As Pa hoped, it was on a bluff, had a good view of the river, trees, and acres for farming.

He had already signed the papers to buy it.

"Have you told Annika yet?" Libby asked.

Pa shook his head. "I've been watching for her. I can hardly wait to tell her."

Seeing her father's excitement, Libby suddenly felt confused. During recent months she had longed for a special woman in her life. Someone she could talk with, not just now and then, but forever. Someone who would be a wife for Pa, a mother to her. But now Libby wondered, *What will happen to me if Annika and Pa do get married?*

Libby tried to push her worried thoughts aside. *Of course Pa will still love me.*

But Libby's uneasiness wouldn't go away. Still feeling concerned, she went out on the hurricane deck. While she, too, watched for Annika, Libby noticed an artist set up his easel at the edge of the river. When Libby went down to watch, Caleb found her there.

"Let's go visit the Democratic and Republican conventions."

"Will they let us in?"

Caleb shrugged. "We'll find out."

Already the artist had sketched the outline of the *Christina*. The tall white steamboat with its many decks and railings shone in the sunlight. Behind the boat, the high bluffs on the other side of the river ended in a bright blue sky.

As Libby and Caleb started past, the artist turned. For a moment he studied their faces. "Do you live on the *Christina*? Would you like to be part of the picture?"

"Would I!" Libby exclaimed. She wanted any chance she could to see an artist work.

Caleb started to slip away, but the artist called him back. "You too. How about it?"

It wasn't hard to guess how Caleb felt, but Libby was already in place. The artist moved them around until they stood with the *Christina* in the background. As the artist painted, a crowd gathered around him. The artist kept on, looking up only enough to study Libby and Caleb again.

At first Libby stood without moving. She found it fun to be part of the painting. Before long she felt the heat of the afternoon sun. Then she started to itch. The minute she tried to scratch her nose, the artist called out, "Don't move!"

Just then Libby looked beyond the artist. Annika was walking across the levee with Oliver White. Feeling sick, Libby nudged Caleb. Trying not to move her lips, she whispered, "There's Annika!"

Tall and handsome, Oliver White looked down at Annika, his blue eyes smiling into hers. Annika looked up, talking and laughing as if with a good friend.

"Uh-huh," Caleb said, not moving his lips at all.

Libby's stomach tightened. *What if Annika loves Oliver White? What if he upsets all of Pa's hopes and dreams?*

"Hold it!" the artist called out. "Don't change your expression. I'm almost done."

Using all her willpower, Libby forced herself to be still.

"Thank you, thank you," the artist said as he finished up. "I'm traveling up the St. Croix River to Taylors Falls. When I go into Wisconsin, this painting will help me get work."

Against the white background of the *Christina*, Caleb's blond hair stood out. The artist had caught the best of Caleb—the way he held his head when he was sure of where he was going. More than once Libby had seen that look when Caleb took on a dangerous role in the Underground Railroad.

Libby felt even more surprised by the way the artist painted her. In the warmth of the day, soft wisps of hair curled around her face. Something in her face caught Libby up short. From her own training as an artist, Libby knew what it was.

The unhappy look she once had around her eyes was gone. *I care about people now. I care about being part of a never-give-up family.*

As Annika and Mr. White reached the *Christina*, Peter came down the gangplank with Wellington trailing behind him. Taking one look at Mr. White, the dog planted his spindly legs and barked.

When the man tried to pass him, Wellington danced around, blocking the way.

Trying to ignore the terrier, Mr. White started once more for the gangplank. Wellington growled. Mr. White stepped back and glared at Peter. "Get that dog away from me!"

Peter didn't need to hear the man's words. Reaching down, Peter scooped up Wellington in his arms. "I'm sorry, sir," Peter said politely, but Libby knew him well.

Peter feels the way I do. He doesn't want Annika and Mr. White together.

Afraid for Pa and all that could happen, Libby hurried past Annika and Mr. White. When she reached the hurricane deck, she knelt down at the railing that overlooked the main deck. It wasn't long before Libby saw Annika. In each hand she carried a carpetbag.

Uh-oh! Libby thought. *She's ready to move out.*

Libby stood up, ready to run after the teacher. Then Libby noticed Pa. For a moment he talked with Annika. Taking her carpetbags, Pa led her toward the stairs.

By the time they walked up two flights to the hurricane deck, Libby was kneeling out of sight. Closer to the wall of the texas, she could hear every word they said.

When Pa and Annika sat down in two chairs, Libby risked a look around the corner. From her place on the floor of the deck, Libby saw their backs and the sides of their faces. Unless they turned around, they wouldn't see her.

Pleased with her front row seat, Libby settled in to watch and listen.

13

Libby's Big Fumble

$\mathcal{A}$nnika's face glowed with excitement. "I was just coming to thank you for everything. Harriet found me exactly the job I need!"

But Pa looked upset. "I wanted to talk with you again about teaching on the *Christina*."

Annika barely seemed to hear him. "Remember that day when you asked Libby and the boys what they wanted most in life? That was when I felt certain that God wanted me in St. Paul this winter."

Oh no! Libby thought. *Pa can't stay here.* Locked in the frozen North, he would miss at least five months of shipping. Downstream, in warmer waters, he could work much longer.

And with Pa away . . . Libby didn't want to think about all the men in St. Paul who would like to marry a woman such as Annika. *By the time we see her again, she could be an old married woman.*

Libby corrected herself. *Not old. But married. Still beautiful and fun.*

Libby tried to name it. *Still full of heart. Annika cares about people.*

Now Pa asked, "*I* helped you decide to stay in St. Paul?"

"Remember what you said about people who want to help others shape their lives into something good? I can help the people who are already here and the immigrants who come. I can help fugitives like Jordan who want to learn to read and write. I'm a good teacher, Nathaniel. A very good teacher."

"I have no doubt that you are," Pa said softly. "But I can't stay here with you. I have no choice but to get these furs down the river and off to Europe. I need to finish my work downstream and come back up with supplies for winter."

Pa sighed. "Once the river closes with ice, St. Paul is shut off from the rest of the world. The mail that goes in or out is carried by sleigh. We might not hear from each other for months at a time!"

"I know," Annika said. "Everyone has warned me about the winters." Her eyes were soft, as if she, too, longed to board the *Christina*, to be part of the family that traveled up and down the river together.

"I'd like to be with you, Nathaniel. I'd like to teach Libby, Caleb, Jordan, and Peter. But the Lord wants me here this winter."

"I won't even know if you're all right!"

"You'll know," Annika said gently. "The Lord will tell you if I'm not all right. He'll speak to me the same way about you."

For a time Pa was silent. Finally he asked, "There's nothing I can say to make you change your mind?"

Annika thought for a moment. "It would have to be God who changes my mind."

"Has He told you why you are to stay here?"

"If I came on board now, it would be too soon."

Pa ran his fingers through his hair. "I didn't mean to get married now. I meant to give us time to get to know each other. To allow me, if I may, to court you, to show you how much you mean to me."

Annika smiled. "I would like to be courted by you. To feel as though I'm the most special woman on earth. But it's too soon."

"For me? For you?"

"For Libby. If I came to stay on the *Christina* now, she would think she got her way. She wants a mother. Snap her fingers. Poof! Like magic, she has one."

"I see," said Pa.

"It's a serious thing to take on a new member of a family. Libby isn't ready for a mother yet. She's still getting used to having Peter for a brother."

"How I can help her?"

"I don't know. But when the time comes, *you'll* know."

A look of pain crossed Pa's face. "Right now the river is my life and my work. But a time will come when railroads will replace steamboats. I have another dream for when that happens. I wanted to take you there, to show you my dream. A home on top of a bluff, land around it for farming, and timber too. But—"

Pa stopped. Annika was part of the dream, and now, perhaps *not* a part.

For a long moment Pa gazed into her eyes. Reaching out, he took her hand.

"Annika, is there someone else you love? Someone here in St. Paul?"

Annika looked down, her long lashes dark against the soft color of her cheeks. When she looked up again, her eyes held the mischief that Libby recognized. "You mean Mr. Oliver White? It's true we have a lot in common. We both like music."

Then Annika met Pa's gaze, and her voice changed. "The man of my dreams won't be here in St. Paul."

Pa shrank back. "Who is he? Where will he be?"

"He'll be on the *Christina*, somewhere on the Mississippi River, far south of here."

Pa smiled. "I'll be very glad if it stays that way." Once more he looked deep into her eyes. When he bent his head, his lips brushed Annika's cheek.

"There's something I want you to remember," he said when he lifted his head. His voice was strong, but Libby heard the tears at the edge of it. "Wherever I am, I'll be thinking of you."

"And I will be praying for you," Annika promised.

Pa stood up slowly, but then walked quickly away, not looking back.

When Annika also left, Libby slipped out from her hiding place. One part of her felt angry. *Oh, Annika! How can you be so stubborn? How can you be so sure that God wants you here this winter?*

For the first time, Libby almost hated Annika's beliefs because of the way they kept her from being with Pa. *Just when things were really going well! Just when she and Pa seem to like each other!*

Then something else weighed on Libby. *Why does she think I'm not ready for a mother? That I'm still getting used to a brother? Who does Annika think I am—a spoiled child? I'm not that way anymore!*

Taking the long way around the texas, Libby walked to her room. She found Annika looking for her. "I wanted to say good-bye," the teacher said.

Libby swallowed around the lump in her throat. She wanted to ask Annika a hundred questions, but she knew she couldn't. Annika would know she had listened in.

"I'll miss you," Libby said instead, her voice small and quiet.

"I'll miss you too." For a moment Annika stood there, waiting until Libby looked into her eyes. "Whatever happens to you in life, you are a very special child of God."

After a quick hug, Annika was gone, and Libby felt empty deep inside. When Samson flopped onto the deck, Libby sat down next to him. As she scratched behind the dog's ears, Libby wished she could forget Annika's last words. *It sounds as if she's saying good-bye forever.*

For a long time Libby brushed Samson's coat. "I'm glad I have you," Libby whispered at last. "Life is simpler with you."

The sun had set, and darkness covered the waterfront as the *Christina* prepared to leave St. Paul. All of the freight and most of the passengers were on board. Libby stood high on the hurricane deck, looking toward Jackson Street.

I'm going to miss you, St. Paul, she thought. In the few short days she had been there, Libby had started to love the city. *It's like Pa said. There are good people here. Kind people.*

Then as she peered into the night, all of her warmhearted feelings changed.

Coming along Jackson Street was a short man wearing a business suit and hat. He carried a gold-headed cane and headed straight toward the *Christina*.

Dread tightened Libby's stomach. *Is that really Riggs?* Since seeing the man in St. Anthony, she had been afraid of this. In a few minutes she felt sure. It was Jordan's owner, all right.

Libby raced for the stairs. By the time she found Jordan in the engine room, she was badly frightened and out of breath.

"You've got to hide," she told him. "Riggs is coming on board! I think the pawnshop owner tipped him off. Riggs must know you're here."

Jordan sighed. "I reckon he does. I'll make sure I stay out of sight."

As the *Christina* left St. Paul, Libby told Pa about Riggs.

"That's fine." Pa wasn't at all upset. "As long as we know where he is, we can keep an eye on him."

That night when Libby woke up, she ached inside. Like a nightmare, her first thought stayed with her. *Annika isn't with us. She stayed behind.*

Libby tried to push the thought away, but another crowded in. *She said I'm not ready for a mother. It's all my fault!*

In the morning Pa called them together for school. So Jordan could be with them, they met in the cargo area, in a hidden room made with tall piles of freight. A lantern close beside them, Caleb wrote for Peter. When they asked about Annika, Libby suspected that all of them missed her as much as she did.

"The speculators want land for the money it will bring them," Libby said when Pa asked what they learned in St. Paul. "For immigrants, land is something more. They want land to make a home—to begin a new way of life."

Caleb and Jordan had managed to learn about the conventions held by the men working to create a new state. Jordan reported on that. "The new Republican party wants to give men like my daddy the right to vote!"

"Does everyone in Minnesota want that?" Pa asked.

Jordan grinned. "No, sir. Can't say that they do. Some of those people are putting up a mighty big fight."

For the first time since leaving Annika, Pa laughed. "When we get to Galena, what are you going to tell your parents, Jordan?"

"That wherever we live, there are goin' to be things to make us afraid. But if we live where God wants us, we can ask for His protection. We can fight to be free. I is going to fight—"

Jordan stopped and corrected himself. "I am goin' to fight by gettin' educated. Mr. Thompson says I need to let myself be free."

Let myself be free? Libby thought. Again she wondered, *What does that mean?*

When class was over, Pa asked Libby to stay for a minute. With the lantern set on the floor between them, Pa asked, "How are you doing, Libby?"

Libby decided to be honest. "It bothers me that you left Annika behind."

"I didn't have any choice," Pa said. "If I really love Annika, I need to believe she is able to hear God—to make the choices He wants her to make. If I don't respect her beliefs, we can't build our love on the strong foundation where I want it."

"But doesn't it scare you?" Libby asked. "Aren't you afraid she'll fall in love with Oliver White?"

"Yes, Libby, I am. But Annika has to follow God's leading in her life. I need to do the same thing. Right now God seems to be leading us in two different directions. Annika believes she is to stay. I need to leave."

"But everything is left unfinished!" Libby wailed. "We didn't find the stolen violin. We haven't figured out the fiddler's secret. You don't know what will happen with Annika." Inside, Libby felt angry. "Is it like God to leave things unfinished?"

Pa smiled. "No, Libby, it isn't. Right now it doesn't make sense. But we have to give God time."

When she met Pa's eyes, there was something Libby knew. *He feels the loss of Annika for my sake as well as his.*

For a moment Libby felt better. Then she remembered the promise Pa gave them the day Annika came to class. *All things work together for good for those who love you? For those who are called according to your purpose?*

If that's true, what's your purpose for me?

As she thought about it, Libby remembered her desire to be strong, even in the hard times. *Lord, do you want me to be strong in you?*

Pa broke into Libby's thoughts. "There's something else I've been wanting to talk with you about. How would you feel about making Peter an official part of our family?"

"You mean adopt him?"

Pa nodded. "I wanted to wait—to talk with Annika first. But I don't know if our choice will affect her. Peter needs a family now."

Afraid to meet Pa's eyes, Libby looked down. A part of her felt scared—scared right down to her toes. *What if Pa changes? What if he doesn't have time for me anymore?*

It didn't help that Peter trailed Pa around, spending time with Pa any chance he got. Every time Libby wanted to talk with Pa, Peter was there.

Folding and unfolding the cloth of her skirt, Libby tried to think how to ask what she wanted to know. Then, like a stream of water dammed up for too long, her words tumbled out. "If you adopt Peter, what will happen to me?"

"Remember how we talked about being a never-give-up family?" Pa asked.

Libby nodded. She had asked Pa for such a family after one of the most awful moments of her life. "How could I ever forget?"

"We agreed that you and I are that family. We said that people living with us on the *Christina* could also be part of that family— a wider family. Remember how I told you that I love Caleb as a son?"

"Yes," Libby answered. At one time that had bothered her.

"I love Peter the same way. And Annika and I are growing in our friendship with each other."

Libby swallowed hard. *I wanted to be strong and I'm not.* She truly wanted Pa and Annika to get married. Yet Libby still felt mixed up about that too. *Will Pa change? Will he have time for me?*

As though hearing her thoughts, Pa kept on. "When I open my heart and life to these people, my love just gets bigger. They don't take your place in my life. There is no one—absolutely no one—who can do that."

"Will you love me just the same?" Libby asked.

"Always. Forever. Unconditionally. In spite of what you do or don't do."

Libby searched Pa's eyes. His face was filled with love but also the honesty she had learned to trust.

"I believe you, Pa," Libby said softly. "With all my heart I believe you."

"And Peter? What should we do?"

In that moment Libby understood. "He needs to know you're his pa, just like I need to know it."

Libby reached up for a hug, and Pa's arms went around her.

During lunch, the tables in the main cabin were set closer than usual because of the number of passengers returning to their homes in the South. Even the captain's table was crowded next to one wall.

Libby sat between her pa and Aunt Vi. As always, Vi wore her Sunday go-to-meeting clothes. In spite of the August heat, she had a short jacket over her dress. Still hoping to turn Libby into a proper young lady, Vi was making her more uncomfortable by the moment.

"Libby, have you forgotten how to hold your fork?"

Each time her aunt corrected her, Libby did her best. Soon she fumbled with nervousness.

When the steward tried to hand Vi a bowl of gravy, he was unable to reach her. Libby offered to help. As she took the bowl, her hand slipped, and the gravy spilled onto her aunt's jacket.

Instantly Vi jumped up. "Oh, Libby! How can you!"

Libby was horrified. "Quick! Take it off so it doesn't burn you." Libby helped her aunt out of the jacket.

Vi was unharmed but very angry. "Libby Norstad, you are thirteen years old and still clumsy. This is a new jacket!"

Libby's face burned with shame. "Let me take it," she said. "I'll wash it right away." *And I'll get out of here too*, Libby promised herself, eager to escape.

In the women's room, Libby filled a bowl with water, then added soap. Before washing the jacket she checked the pockets. When Libby found a folded slip of paper, she opened it.

> *Captain Norstad—*
> *It will stay that way.*
> *A.*

Libby couldn't believe her eyes. She remembered Pa telling Annika, *"I'll be very glad if it stays that way."* And here it was, Annika's answer!

The minute she found Pa alone, Libby gave the note to him.

"Captain Norstad!" Pa exclaimed. "I know that some women call their husbands mister all their lives. But I thought we had gotten beyond that!"

"Pa," Libby started, then stopped. *If I say something, he'll know I listened in.* She debated what to do. Then she decided to risk it. "Pa, I know what her note means. I heard you and Annika talking."

For a moment her father stared at her. "Elizabeth Norstad! You know you shouldn't listen in! That was a private conversation!"

The warm flush of embarrassment rushed into Libby's face. "I'm sorry, Pa. I'm truly sorry. But look what Annika said."

As her father stared down at the note in his hand, hope returned to his eyes. "Good," he said. "Good!"

Carefully he folded the note and put it in an inside pocket of his captain's uniform. "Where did you find this, Libby?"

When she told him, Pa did an about-face and stalked off to his cabin.

14

Danger Stranger!

*A*t the end of the evening meal, Pa spoke to Libby and Aunt Vi. "I want to talk with both of you. I'll meet you in my cabin."

When Libby and her aunt reached Pa's cabin, Vi looked around as if she had never seen it. "This is where you have school?" she asked.

"Pa does a good job of teaching us," Libby answered, always ready to defend her father.

But Vi was already pacing around the room. When she headed for the rocking chair to sit down, Libby spoke quickly. "That's Pa's chair." She couldn't bear to see her aunt sitting in it. Instead, Libby offered one of the chairs at the table.

By the time the silence had grown long between them, Pa appeared. Drawing up his rocking chair, he sat down. "I'm sorry about the problem at lunch today."

"Libby was clumsy again," Vi answered. "She spilled gravy all over my lovely new jacket."

"Can you tell me about it, Libby?" Pa asked.

"Auntie is right," Libby answered. "I was nervous. I spilled."

"And why were you nervous?"

Oh, Pa! Libby wanted to cry out. *You were there. Why do you have to ask?*

When she didn't speak, Pa asked again. "Why were you nervous, Libby?"

With one quick glance, Libby took in her aunt. Her back straight as a stick, she looked prim and proper. Libby knew her aunt expected her to act the same way.

"I was trying to do everything just right." Libby spoke in a low voice.

"What happened that caused you to spill?"

"The tables were set too close together. There wasn't enough room for the steward to get around behind Auntie. I offered to help and my hand slipped. The gravy spilled."

"All over me," Vi said grimly. "I could have been scalded to death."

"All over your thick jacket," Libby said politely. She knew the layers of cloth had protected her aunt. "I offered to wash the jacket."

Vi sniffed. "As any normal person should do."

"And?" Pa asked Libby.

In that moment she understood what he was trying to do. Libby wanted to giggle but knew she had better not. No matter what, she had to keep a straight face.

"I felt bad." Libby did her best to sound sorry. "I wanted to be sure I did everything right. So I checked the pockets before I washed the jacket."

"Did you find anything in the pockets?" Pa asked.

Libby's gaze met Pa's. "I found a note addressed to you."

"Oh," Pa said. "That's a strange place to find a note addressed to me. How do you think it got there?"

Libby shrugged. "Maybe Auntie would know."

Only then did Libby risk a glance that way. Her aunt's face seemed frozen. The next instant it thawed with a red flush that covered her cheeks.

"When did you get the note?" Pa asked Vi, giving no hint how important the message was to him.

"Just before we left St. Paul." Vi stumbled, clearly embarrassed. "Annika ran up to the boat. A very improper lady she is."

"She asked for me?"

"Yes. I told her you were gone, so she gave me the note."

"But I wasn't gone," Pa said. "Why did you tell her that?"

Vi swallowed hard. "I was sure you wouldn't want to be bothered with such a young lady."

"I wouldn't want to be bothered with Annika?" Pa's voice held a sound that made Libby tremble. "Did you say that to her?"

"Oh no, of course not. I would never be so rude." But Vi's eyes wavered, and Libby knew her aunt was lying.

"You simply told her I never wanted to see her again."

As if Pa had come too close to the truth, Vi blushed. "Did Libby tell you that?" she blurted out.

Pa's face was white now with a look more desperate than Libby had ever seen. "You actually told her I never wanted to see her again?"

Her gaze still on Pa, Vi leaned back in her chair. "No, I didn't. I told Annika that if she married you, she would always be second best."

"Second best?" Pa roared. "What did you mean by that?"

"That you would always love my sister, Christina, more."

Pa looked stunned. "I can't believe you said that! Why? And why didn't you give me the note?"

"I forgot." Vi's eyes wavered again.

"You forgot. For one whole night and morning you forgot." With angry steps Pa paced around the cabin, then sat down again. "Why? Why did you do this?"

As Libby watched, her aunt's eyes filled with resentment. "If you marry Annika, you'll have an excuse to keep Libby on this awful boat. You know this is not the place for a young lady to be. If you want Libby to turn out right, to be a proper society girl, she needs to live in Chicago with me."

Pa leaped to his feet. "You believe I would allow Libby to live with you?" With two giant steps he stood directly in front of Vi, staring into her face. "You think I would make that mistake again?"

Just as suddenly Pa backed away. When he spoke, his voice sounded so calm that Libby knew he was holding tight to his control.

"In two hours we'll reach Galena," he told Vi. "You can stay at the DeSoto House tonight. Tomorrow you can take a stage-coach or connect with a train to Chicago. Pack your many bags and be ready to go."

Suddenly Vi assumed the air of a queen. "My dear dead sister, Libby's mother, would not approve of this."

Pa refused to back down. "My dear Christina, my beloved wife and Libby's mother, would wholeheartedly approve. Now go. Don't let me see your face until you're standing at the gang-plank, ready to get off this boat."

As Vi reached the door, Pa spoke. "Two more questions," he said. "When did Annika give you the note? Before or after you told her she would always be second best?"

"Before."

"And when you told her she would always be second best, what did she say?"

Vi sniffed. "She lifted her head in that way she has. She said, 'Tell the good captain and his Libby good-bye from me.'"

Without another word Vi swept through the door. When Pa closed it firmly behind her, the room was so still that Libby could hear herself breathing.

Pa dropped down in his chair. Elbows on his knees, he braced his head with the palms of his hands. When his shoulders trembled, Libby wrapped her arms around him.

Her father's words cut through to her heart. "Oh, Libby, what should I do?"

As he began to sob, Libby remembered that she hadn't seen Pa weep in that way since her mother died.

When at last he looked up, Libby said, "You could send Annika a telegram."

Pa shook his head. "The telegraph hasn't reached St. Paul."

For a minute Pa sat there, deep in thought. "I'll write the best letter I can," he said at last. "I'll explain everything that hap-pened. I'll tell her that—" Pa broke off.

"That you love her," Libby said softly.

Pa smiled, and his eyes cleared. "That my love for her is a different kind of love than it was for Christina. That my love will be even deeper because I know what it means to lose a wife. Do you understand, Libby?" he asked gently.

Libby wasn't sure that she did. Yet in that moment of seeing Pa weep, her concerns about having a mother had fallen away. She just wanted the best for Pa. "You and Annika could be happy together."

"Yes," Pa agreed. "We could. And you would be a very special part of our happiness."

As Libby left the cabin, Pa took up a pen, ready to fill a clean white sheet of paper.

Near the mouth of the Galena River, Caleb asked Libby to help him know when it would be safe for Jordan to leave the *Christina*.

"Go up on the boiler deck," he said. "Stay close to where Riggs has his room."

In the darkness of night, Libby waited next to the railing. Soon a man stopped nearby. He made Libby jumpy. *In just a few miles—as soon as we reach Galena—Jordan has to leave. How will I know if it's safe for him?*

When the stranger moved closer to Libby, she edged farther away. *I'm on my father's boat,* she told herself. Quickly she glanced around. There were plenty of passengers on the deck. *If I scream I'm okay.*

The stranger looked straight ahead over the river and began speaking.

Libby felt sure he was talking to himself. *What an unusual man!* Then she heard his words.

"I am a slave owner," he said quietly.

Libby's heart leaped into her throat. As she turned to see his face, he said, "Don't look at me. Look down at the water."

His voice was even quieter now. "There's much about being a slave owner that I regret. I tried to set my slaves free. I took them across the river and told them to start a new life. Some of them left, but the next morning many were back. I meant well, but it wasn't enough. All their lives I had forced them to depend on me. I treated them worse than children because I didn't allow them to think. If I was going to set them free, I needed to let them prepare for freedom."

The man cleared his throat. "You have a fugitive on board. A fugitive who knows how to win and use freedom. His name is Jordan."

Libby froze, unwilling to give away by one flick of an eyelash that she knew what he was talking about.

"Jordan is a runaway slave, isn't he?"

Terrified now, Libby swallowed hard. Knotting her hands, she held them tight, afraid that her nervousness would give Jordan away. But the man talked on.

"Jordan's owner is on board. Riggs thinks you'll put Jordan off in Galena. If you want my help I'll give it."

Her heart beating triple time, Libby began to pray. *If I ask questions, he'll know I know about Jordan.* Yet as she stood there praying, one thought came to mind. *Lord, if you want me to trust this man, give him a good plan.*

"If what you're saying is true, how would you distract Riggs?" Libby asked.

"When the boat comes into Galena, I'll start talking about a good business deal—a deal where Riggs would make big money. I'll tell him I have to talk *now* before leaving the *Christina.*"

Libby smiled. The plan was perfect. There was nothing that interested Riggs more than making money. *Maybe that's why he started trading slaves in the first place.*

"Have Jordan leave the minute the gangplank goes out," the man went on. "I'll make sure Riggs is in the main cabin. But I can't promise how long I can keep him if Jordan doesn't leave."

"It's his life if you give him away," Libby said.

"I won't," the man promised. "If you do what I say, Jordan's life is safe with me."

The man turned away. Libby waited until she was sure he was gone. Then she hurried down to the engine room to talk with Caleb and Jordan. When she explained what had happened, Jordan made the choice whether to trust the slave owner.

Jordan went back over Libby's story. "You prayed?" he wanted to know. "You asked the Lord to give the man a good plan?"

As Libby nodded, Jordan grinned. Standing tall, he wore that look of royalty again. "The good Lord told me something. He said, 'Jordan, you trust that man. And you tell Libby she's become a good conductor on the Underground Railroad.' "

When Jordan left the *Christina*, he went as a rouster. Hoisting a small barrel onto his shoulder, he hid his face from anyone on the *Christina* who might watch. From near the gangplank Libby and Caleb watched him walk ashore. Partway across the large area filled with freight, he set down the barrel and walked away.

Just then a shadow rose from behind a big crate. Jordan stopped dead. When a second, then a third shadow rose behind him, Jordan was surrounded.

Caleb leaped to his feet. "Something's wrong!"

With one quick glance, he looked around to see if anyone was watching. In the next instant Caleb hurried down the gangplank with Libby close on his heels. Faster and faster Caleb walked, as though not wanting to attract attention by running.

He and Libby dodged this way and that between people and freight, but Libby kept sight of Jordan. Soon there were four shadows, then five, next to him. By the time Libby and Caleb reached the last pile of freight, seven people stood around Jordan.

Men, Libby thought, glimpsing their size in the darkness. *Slave catchers? After all Jordan has gone through to be free?*

15

The Worst?

*A*s quickly as the men appeared, they disappeared, and Jordan with them. "What happened?" Libby whispered to Caleb.

Before he could answer, she heard a soft whistle. Caleb slowed down, walked a few more steps, then stopped. "Just do what I do."

Next to a pile of barrels sitting on the waterfront, he turned around and looked back to the *Christina*. Libby did the same. The gangplank was flooded with passengers leaving. As Libby watched them, she sensed a movement close behind her.

"Don't look," Caleb warned, still in a whisper.

Five steamboats had tied up along the waterfront. *Five steamboats from where?* Libby wondered. *Are they going south or coming north?*

In that moment Libby guessed why Caleb stood quietly and what the whistled signal meant. Waiting in the darkness, she did not move. Once, she heard the scrape of gravel as if someone wore boots. *Jordan?*

Then she knew. *Bare feet move without sound.*

Within a few minutes, Libby heard the call of a bird. When Caleb turned around, he faced the business area of Galena, and

Libby knew she had recognized another signal. Walking together, she and Caleb hurried up a short flight of steps. At the top was a large building with a sign that read Union House.

Two large porches stretched across the front of the hotel, one on the ground floor and the other on the second. As she and Caleb drew close, Libby saw a man drop onto his knees and crawl under the lower porch.

On the back side of the hotel, Caleb and Libby met Jordan. Even in the shadows, Libby could see the laughter in his face.

"Remember what Riggs told me?" Jordan asked. "That a slave had never escaped from him alive?"

Libby remembered all right. The thought of it still filled her with dread.

But Jordan wiggled his shoulders with glee. "Those men you saw? They came from near where I used to live! Riggs bought them. When they heard I escaped, they thought, 'We is gettin' away too!' All this time they've been figuring out how to do it!"

Caleb's soft laugh filled the darkness. "So you were the beginning!"

Jordan clapped Caleb's shoulder. "Thanks for everything, my friend! I need to leave you now."

They were partway back to the river when Caleb laughed again, then whispered, "It's more than leading his family now. Jordan will be one of the best conductors the Underground Railroad has!"

"Where will he take them?"

Caleb's grin stretched from ear to ear. "To his family, I expect, until it's safe to send them on to Freeport. Wait till Riggs gets home and hears about all the money he's lost. Some sort of justice to that, don't you think?"

As they drew close to the *Christina*, Riggs tore across the front deck. His face red with anger, he looked in every direction.

"He doesn't dare come down here in the darkness," Caleb whispered. "He's afraid to walk between the freight." Finally Riggs whirled around and stalked back up the steps to the main cabin.

When Libby reached the gangplank, she met Pa and Aunt Vi coming down. By now deckhands had set Vi's big trunk and her many pieces of baggage on the levee. Libby was amazed that her aunt had actually gathered everything together in two hours. *She must have been so mad that she just threw it all in!*

Libby held back a giggle. Carefully she made her face straight and stood next to Pa as he said good-bye.

He was quietly polite to Aunt Vi. "Thank you for all you've done for Libby in the past."

Libby took her lead from him. "You've taught me to enjoy music, to be an artist," she said as she reached up to hug her aunt.

Vi felt stiff and did not put her arms around her. Then Libby remembered. *She doesn't like hugs in public. I embarrassed her again.*

"I've asked a man to see you safely on your way," Pa said. "I wish you and Alex well."

As though with the greatest effort, Vi offered her hand. "And you and Libby also." In front of whatever part of the world might be looking at her, no one would know that anything was wrong.

Pa waited long enough for Vi and her baggage to be taken away. Then he spoke to Libby. "I see a captain I trust. If he's going upriver, I'll give him my letter for Annika. I'll ask him to personally take care of it."

When Pa came back, he told Libby the good news. His friend was headed for St. Paul. Within a few days Annika would receive the letter. Everything would be straightened out.

After breakfast the next morning, Pa said to Libby, "Let's get started on Peter's adoption."

They found him in an open area on the levee. "You're just the one I want to see," Peter told Libby. "Go stand by those crates. I'm teaching Wellington secret signs."

When Libby was in place, Peter stood with his arms down at his side. Looking into the dog's eyes, he raised his right arm slightly. Pointing his index finger toward Libby, Peter commanded, "Go get Libby!"

Wellington ran straight for her. Libby dropped to her knees. "Good dog! Good dog!" She offered the treat that Peter slipped her.

As Pa grinned, Peter said, "Let's try one more thing. I want to see if Wellington obeys me with only hand signals."

This time Peter didn't speak his command. Looking into the dog's eyes, he barely lifted his right arm. Wellington's ears pricked up.

Peter pointed toward Libby. Looking neither to the left nor right, Wellington raced straight for her.

"He did it! He did it!" Peter cried. Pa started clapping.

"Next I'm going to teach Wellington to find you even when he doesn't see you," Peter told Libby.

Reaching out, Pa touched Peter's arm in the signal they used to get each other's attention. As soon as Peter looked at him, Pa pointed to Libby, then himself. Crossing his arms across his chest, Pa made the sign for love and pointed to Peter.

Peter pointed to himself, crossed his arms over his chest, and pointed to Pa.

Taking the slate, Pa wrote quickly. "Libby and I want to adopt you. Would you like that?"

Peter's face lit up. "We'd be a real family?"

This time it was Libby's turn to write. "A never-give-up family."

"I'd like that." Peter's words were quiet, but the excitement in his voice told Libby he would like that very much.

"Let's ask a man to start work on it," Pa said.

When the *Christina* reached St. Louis, Libby and Caleb watched Riggs walk down the gangplank. "I wonder how he's going to like the news that seven more slaves have run away," Libby said.

Caleb grinned. "Maybe by now even more slaves have figured out a way to do it."

Later that morning Pa brought a newspaper back to the *Christina*. "The Ohio Life Insurance and Trust Company closed its doors yesterday," he said.

"Closed its doors?" Libby asked. "What does that mean?"

"It went bankrupt," her father explained. "It's an important New York company, and it doesn't have the money it needs to pay its bills. This could mean the start of an economic panic. People get scared and rush to sell property or stocks. We'll have to wait and see what happens."

For the next few weeks, Pa went up and down the river bringing pigs, or bars, of lead from the mines at Galena to St. Louis. Then one day in late September, as they left St. Louis, Libby found Pa at the railing, looking upriver. When she took a place beside him, he said, "Something is wrong with Annika."

"How do you know, Pa?" Libby had also felt uneasy. In fact, she had been praying more than at any time in her life. Several times she had wondered what to do about it.

"It's something I'm sensing deep inside," her father said. "It's as though God is nudging me—telling me to pray even more than usual for Annika. To pray that she finds a home."

That upset Libby. "I thought she had a home—a good place to stay. A job too."

"Yes, she did have both. But I'm wondering what has happened." As though not wanting to say what he was thinking, Pa looked off in the distance.

"What is it, Pa?" Libby asked when he didn't go on.

"I'm wondering how the economic panic has affected her. If I know Annika—" Again he stopped.

"She's independent," Libby said.

"Yes. All over the country, banks are closing. We have the kind of panic I was afraid would come. Because of the amount of speculation in St. Paul, it could be hit especially hard. Since fortunes were made overnight, they could be lost the same way."

"Pa, what are you saying?" Libby felt more upset all the time.

"What if there's no money to pay Annika? If she lost her job, she wouldn't stay where she couldn't pay her room and board. She's too used to being on her own."

Libby agreed. "But if she has no money, where can she go?"

"That's what bothers me," Pa said. "She might be forced to leave St. Paul. If that happens, how will we find her again?"

A lump formed in Libby's throat. With it came a memory of Wellington and how hungry he was when Peter found him. *What if Annika is hungry?*

Libby pushed the thought aside, telling herself that there had to be enough food in Minnesota Territory. But another worry rushed in. *What if Annika gets so poor that she marries someone else?*

It wasn't hard to remember Oliver White III. He seemed to have so much money that even in a panic he'd be rich. If it was possible to buy food, he could give it to Annika. What if she had to depend on him?

"I'll pour on steam," Pa said. "We'll head for Minnesota Territory as fast as we can safely go."

Libby whirled around and hurried to her room. Not for anything in the world would she tell Pa what she was thinking.

On the way upriver, Pa asked Libby to come to his cabin. The morning was bright and beautiful, but Pa looked as serious as Libby had ever seen him.

"I've been waiting to give you something," he said. "I wanted to be sure you were old enough to appreciate it."

From his desk Pa took out something wrapped in a silk cloth. As he unfolded the cloth, Libby saw the worn leather covers of a book that had been carefully handled but much used.

"It's your mother's Bible," Pa said as he handed it to Libby.

As Libby took it, she felt like crying. It had meant so much to receive her mother's cross and know all that it meant to her parents. Libby couldn't believe that Pa was also giving her Ma's Bible.

"Ma read from this every day?" Libby asked. Only then did she realize how much she had grown since coming to live with Pa.

She tried to explain. "Once, I was silly enough to think a special green dress was my most treasured possession. Now this will be."

With Pa's gaze upon her, Libby carefully opened the Bible. Many of the pages were marked with underlining. Next to the verses, notes and dates had been written in the margins.

"You'll find it's a history of your mother's thoughts," Pa said. "A spiritual history of times when she learned and grew. Times when she suffered and times when she celebrated. Times when she especially recognized the goodness of God."

When Libby was unable to speak, Pa went on. "You'll come to know your mother through these pages, Libby. Even more, you'll grow in knowing the Lord she loved and served."

Long after Pa left, Libby searched the pages of her mother's Bible. When she came to the eighth chapter of Romans, she saw that verse twenty-eight was underlined. *Pa's verse*, Libby thought. *But Ma's too.*

> And we know that all things work together for good to them that love God, to them who are the called according to his purpose.

Reading the words, Libby's questioning heart cried out. *If we love God*, all *things work together for* good?

How could anything good come out of Annika's staying in St. Paul? Now Pa wondered if she even had enough to eat!

Just thinking about it made Libby feel angry. *Aren't you supposed to love us, God? So what about the* all things, *then?*

Then Libby saw that the page was spotted. In those places the paper had drawn together where tears may have fallen. *Did Ma weep as she read that verse?*

Her words seemed to be written in giant letters.

In everything.

I trust you to work in everything.

I think I finally understand, Libby told herself. *Even if things aren't perfect, God can work to bring something good.*

In the margin alongside, Libby saw words written in a small, neat hand: *Lord, you know I don't want to leave my precious daughter, Elizabeth. But I trust you to work in everything, to bring something good, even out of that.*

When Libby began weeping, she could not stop. Hugging the Bible to herself, she repeated the words to which her mother had clung.

As Libby finally wiped the tears from her eyes, there was something she knew. *I can't make grown-ups do something just because I want it. But I already have a never-give-up family—with or without Annika.*

Pa and Caleb and Gran, Libby thought. *Peter.*

A smile flitted across her face. *Even Samson and Wellington.*

Right from the start, Pa had talked about their family being one that would stick together no matter what happened. *It's like belonging to God*, Libby thought, filled with awe. *With God I belong to a never-give-up family. He never gives up on me.*

In that moment Libby began to trust God to take care of Annika. To believe that God could bring something good.

As she lifted her head, she heard a knock on the door.

"Libby!" Caleb called. "Are you all right?"

Still clutching the Bible, Libby opened the door. Caleb's gaze searched her face.

"I'm all right now," she answered. "Just a minute." Returning to Pa's rocker, Libby picked up the silk scarf and wrapped her mother's Bible. Gently she set it inside the drawer until she could read it again.

Out on the deck, Caleb studied her face. "Are you sure you're all right?"

Libby nodded. At first she was afraid to tell him what had happened. Then she knew how much she needed to talk.

"Pa gave me my mother's Bible," Libby said.

As Caleb waited, she made herself go on. "I found Romans 8:28 and something Ma wrote about me. Even though she was dying, she asked God to bring something good out of it."

Once again tears welled up in Libby's eyes. "I'm not very strong, am I? Do you think I'll ever learn to trust God when it's really hard?"

Caleb's gaze met hers. For a moment he looked away, as though unable to say what he thought. Then he seemed to know how much it had cost her to be honest. "You'll learn, Libby. You've changed already. You aren't the same girl who came to live on the *Christina*."

Libby smiled. It was the highest praise Caleb could give her.

Only then did Libby realize that the *Christina* had tied up at Savanna, a small settlement along the river. Near shore, the ground was flat and the buildings not far from the water. Behind the town, limestone bluffs stood tall, rising straight up as if reaching for the sky.

"Peter says he wants to be an explorer, so why don't we take him exploring?" Caleb asked. "Maybe you need some fun too."

The September sun was warm, the air crisp, and the sky bright blue. The idea of being out in that kind of weather made Libby feel good all over.

Then Caleb told her, "Your pa has business that will keep him here for three or four hours. He said it's okay if we hike up the bluff."

"To the top?" Libby felt weak just thinking about it. *Has Caleb forgotten my fear of heights?*

"Remember the view at Hannibal?" he asked. "I'll show you another great view. You'll see up and down the river for miles."

It was always fun being with Caleb, but Libby still felt afraid. Caleb seemed to guess her thoughts.

"You'll like it, Libby. Really you will."

As he filled his knapsack, Libby watched. A coil of rope. An extra shirt. Two light jackets. Strips of cloth rolled for bandages.

"Get a sweater, and I'll carry it for you," Caleb told her.

When Libby returned with the sweater, Caleb stuffed it inside his knapsack. Already he had filled three canteens of water. In a leather case attached to his belt he put a sharp knife.

"What's that for?" Libby asked.

Caleb shrugged. "The unexpected. That's the way your pa trained me. 'Be ready for the worst,' he said. 'Be glad if you don't need it.' "

The worst? Libby wondered. Afraid she would sound like a scaredy-cat, she didn't ask what that meant. *A bear? A wolf?*

16

Nasty Surprise

*C*aleb closed his knapsack. "We'll pick up sandwiches from Gran. As soon as we find Peter, we can go."

The ten-year-old was on the main deck. When Caleb pointed to himself, Libby, and the bluff, Peter understood. Caleb settled the knapsack on his back, and the three of them set out at once.

At first the climb was easy, and they passed quickly between the few trees left on the lower hillside. Steamboat crews had cut off huge areas of timber to feed the hungry furnaces that heated water in the boilers. When Caleb came to an area of long grass, he stopped them

"Keep your eyes open," he warned them. "Watch where you step." Taking the slate Peter carried, Caleb wrote, "Copperhead snakes."

Libby swallowed hard. If Caleb wanted to show her a good view, she wanted to see it. But she didn't care to see a snake.

Peter's eyes widened. "Poisonous, you mean?"

Caleb nodded. Again he wrote. "Timber rattlesnakes too."

"How will we know?" Peter asked.

"Listen for the rattle," Caleb answered without thinking. "Back off if you hear it."

A moment later Caleb muttered an "Uh-oh!" as if suddenly

remembering Peter's deafness. Caleb took the slate again.

"Watch," Caleb wrote and drew a rock with a coiled snake sitting on top of it, then another snake peering out of tall grass. Next to that he drew the tail of a snake with five or six rattles sticking up on the end.

Peter grinned, and his blue eyes lit up. "I'd like to see a rattler. I'd really be an explorer then." The possibility of snakes didn't bother him at all, but even the thought filled Libby with dread.

When they started out again, Caleb took the lead, with Peter second and Libby third. Caleb didn't need to remind Libby to listen for Peter.

The bluff was steeper now, and Caleb led them in zigzag slants, changing direction often to take the easiest slope. Above the area where steamboat crews had cut, there were trees again. By now the muscles in Libby's legs ached from the steep climb, and she welcomed the shade.

Soon large masses of limestone broke through the soil. Climbing between boulders, they grabbed small trees and branches to pull themselves up. At last they came out at the top of the bluff.

As if offering a big gift, Caleb led Libby and Peter to a ledge overlooking the river. Far below them the river widened, stretching out to the western horizon. Both upstream and down Libby could see for miles. Best of all, she could see the *Christina*.

"Oh, look!" Peter exclaimed when he peered down on the steamboat. "See how long it is? How it shines in the sun? It's like a toy boat I used to have!"

Even from here Libby could see the tall smokestacks, the white railings, the pilothouse perched on top. Peter was right. It did look like a toy small enough to push around in a springtime puddle. Instead, the *Christina* was surrounded by blue water sparkling in the sun.

Forgetting her fear of heights, Libby caught her breath at the beauty of it. Peter was even more excited.

"I feel like Lewis and Clark or Zebulon Pike, or one of the other explorers I learned about in school! We need to plant a flag up here!"

Far overhead, the sun had edged past its midpoint. Caleb took out sandwiches, and they sat down on the warm rock ledges to eat. Libby felt good. She had climbed to the top. She hadn't shamed herself by showing panic about the heights. Best of all, they had given Peter a good time.

When they started off again, Caleb led them with Peter not far behind. As the heels of Libby's shoes dug into the steep slope, limestone crumbled into small pieces. A rock broke away and tumbled down the bluff.

Caleb stopped. "Careful," he warned. "Walk where I walk."

When Caleb pointed to Peter's feet, then his own, Peter got the message. His grin told Libby this was the greatest adventure he'd ever had.

Farther on, the going was steep. Peter followed Caleb from one rock ledge to the next. Between the shelves, water had raced down the bluff, creating a path.

They had walked for a time when Caleb dropped behind a boulder. When he came into view farther on, Peter started taking a different way.

"Peter!" Libby called out, forgetting he couldn't hear. "Stay in Caleb's path!" Then Libby remembered, and she hurried to warn him. Before she could catch up, Libby heard a sound.

At first she thought it was steam escaping. *How can I hear the* Christina *so far away?*

Like dry leaves blown before a wind, the sound came again. In that moment Libby knew. The whirring sound of a rattle.

"Peterrrr!" Libby screamed.

Caleb whirled around, his face white. Leaping from ledge to ledge, he raced back up the bluff.

Sliding on the loose stones of the washouts, Libby took the shortest way down. She had nearly caught up to Peter when she saw the wide ledge just below him. A large snake with black rings lay coiled, ready to spring. Tail up, it rattled again.

As Peter's foot came down on the ledge, the snake's head leaped out. Its fangs sank deep in Peter's leg.

Peter screamed. Looking down, he froze. Libby grabbed his arm and yanked him back. The snake slithered away. Moments later it disappeared beneath a rock ledge.

Caleb took one look at Peter's leg and caught him up in his arms. When Caleb laid him down in an open space, Peter moaned. "It stings! It stings!"

Kneeling on the ground beside him, Libby stared at Peter's leg. Puncture marks showed where the fangs of the rattlesnake had sunk into his flesh.

Caleb tore open his knapsack, pulled out strips of cloth, and layered them one on top of another. With quick, sure movements he tied the tourniquet around Peter's leg above the wound. Then he yanked the knife from his belt.

Lighting a match, Caleb ran the flame along the edges of the blade. A second and third time he lit matches, making sure the blade was clean.

"Hold his legs for me," Caleb ordered as he knelt down opposite Libby. "You better pray at the same time."

Already the flesh around the wound had started to swell and change color. As though to say, "Okay, Peter, get ready," Caleb clasped his shoulder.

For an instant Caleb held the knife above the wound. Then he cut through the fang mark, opening the flesh.

Peter jerked. Libby's stomach turned over.

"Hold him again." When Caleb cut open the second fang mark, Peter moaned. Paying no attention, Caleb bent over the wounds.

As Libby realized what he was going to do, she cried out, "Oh no! You'll die too!"

"Don't let go!" Caleb answered. "Hang on to him!" With his mouth on the first wound, Caleb sucked at the opening, turned his head, and spit out the blood.

Libby gagged. But Caleb bent down again, sucked at the second wound, and spit out the blood.

Again Libby gagged. Then the horror of it struck her. *Caleb is giving his life! I can't throw up. I can't!*

Looking away, she stared at Peter's face. His eyes wide with fear, Peter stared back at her. In that instant Libby's nausea vanished.

Letting go of his legs, Libby squeezed Peter's hand. Peter blinked, caught for one moment by something greater than fear. Crossing her arms across her chest, Libby signed, "I love you."

A ghost of a smile crossed Peter's face. Then he squeezed his eyes tight and balled his fists into knots, trying to close out the pain.

After sucking the wounds again, Caleb loosened the tourniquet. A minute later he tightened the band. "Water, Libby. Give him a little water."

With shaking hands, Libby opened a canteen. As she held it to Peter's lips and lifted his head, one thought filled her mind. *What if both of them die up here?*

"We've got to get Peter down the bluff." Caleb's voice was strained. "We've got to keep his head higher than his leg. He can't walk or the poison will spread even more."

Standing up, Caleb looked down the rest of the bluff. They had nearly reached the end of the rocks, but the way was still steep and long.

Peter's face was pale now, his eyes frightened again. When Libby tried to comfort him, she found his hand cold and clammy. Opening the knapsack, she pulled out her sweater.

As she helped Peter into it, he asked, "Libby, am I going to die?"

Libby shook her head and kept shaking it till she thought it would fall off.

"Libby, are you telling the truth?"

Libby nodded her head several times.

"That's good," Peter said. "But if I do die, will you take care of Wellington?"

Libby groaned. After all her impatience with the dog, now he was the one Peter thought about?

Then Libby felt ashamed. "Yes, Peter." Making the sign for Wellington's name, she nodded her head. To make sure Peter believed her, she held up her hand and signed, "I promise."

Locking their arms and hands together, Libby and Caleb made a chair between them. With Peter's arms around their necks, they set out.

At the steepest place Caleb stopped, loosened and then tightened the tourniquet, and prayed for Peter. When they went on again, Libby kept repeating the name of Jesus. At last the *Christina* came into sight.

Afterward Libby never knew how they got down the bluff. She only remembered her terrible fear that she would drop Peter. That he would land on his bad leg. That he would die before they reached the *Christina*. And through it all came a nagging fear. *What will happen to Caleb?*

The minute Pa saw them on the cut-over area of the bluff, he gave the order to get the steam up. Then he and three other men hurried to meet them. As they carried Peter up the gangplank, the crew was already untying the lines. Moments later the *Christina* put out into the river.

With the engineer pouring on steam, they headed up the Mississippi. "There's a marine hospital in Galena," Pa explained. "A hospital owned by the Public Health Service to take care of people working on boats. If we can get there in time—"

Pa broke off. "Caleb, you did all the right things." His eyes filling with tears, Pa started to shake his hand. Instead, Pa's arms went around Caleb in a big bear hug.

For the first time since the rattlesnake struck, Caleb crumpled. Like a little boy needing comfort, Caleb stood within Pa's arms and cried.

Again Libby felt ashamed. *Caleb, I wondered if you were real. You've had to be real so many times, you don't even know you're a hero.*

The rest of the way up the river, Libby, Pa, Caleb, and Gran took turns sitting beside Peter. In the few minutes she and her father were alone with him, Libby told Pa her terrible fear.

"Caleb sucked out the blood and poison. Can he die too?"

"I asked Caleb if he had any cuts in his mouth," Pa said quietly. "He doesn't think so."

"That's what would make the difference?"

"There's a lot we don't know, but I think so." Pa sighed. "I love Caleb like a son, and I love Peter the same way."

As if Pa was trying to shake all the weight off his shoulders, he smiled. "We're getting to be more and more of a family, aren't we, Libby?"

"A never-give-up family." Libby tried to smile, too, but she didn't quite make it.

In Galena they took Peter to the marine hospital set on the hill across the river from the business area. Standing outside, Libby looked up at the beautiful brick building. Wide verandas, or porches, wrapped around both floors. On the top of the roof was a white cupola. The scared feeling at the pit of Libby's stomach wouldn't go away.

Dr. Newhall echoed Pa's words to Caleb. "If you had a doctor's training, you couldn't have done better."

Pa told Libby more about Horatio Newhall. Long ago he had started the first store for selling medicines in the state of Illinois. He also started the first newspaper in Galena, the *Miners' Journal*. Listening to Pa, Libby felt hopeful. Then she learned that if someone didn't die of snakebite right away, he could still die later—weeks later.

It was as though Peter had a case of blood poisoning. Day after day Libby, Caleb, Pa, and Gran visited him in the brick hospital at the top of the hill. Day after day Jordan and Serena came to see him. Everyone who knew Peter prayed for him. Yet six weeks after the rattlesnake's bite, he seemed no better, only worse.

"Will you write to my school?" Peter asked Libby one day. "My friends will wonder why I didn't come when school started after harvest."

Libby did as he asked and wrote to the school for the deaf in Jacksonville, Illinois. Halfway through the letter she started crying. *Will Peter ever see his friends again?*

As one week slipped into another, Pa seemed thinner every day. Finally Libby asked him, "You're worried about Peter, aren't you?"

"Abscesses have formed," Pa told her. "Pockets of infection near the fang marks, but also in other parts of his body."

"And you're worried about Annika too?" Libby knew Pa wouldn't leave for a city as far away as St. Paul when Peter was so ill.

"Not worried," Pa said. "Concerned. I feel more peaceful about her now. But I wish I knew what was happening to Annika. I've sent at least five letters upriver. Why doesn't she answer? With each letter I told her how to reach me in Galena."

Pa sighed. "If only I could telegraph, or hear from her, or find someone who has seen her—"

"You've never heard a word from steamboat captains?" Libby asked, though she felt she knew the answer.

Pa shook his head. "If Annika is in St. Paul, she must wonder why I haven't returned. She might even wonder if I keep my word."

"Annika knows you keep your promises," Libby said. But then she wondered, *What were Pa's promises?* As far as she knew, a promise of marriage had never been made between them.

With dread Libby remembered Annika's last words to Aunt Vi: *"Tell the good captain and his Libby good-bye from me."* Worse still, Libby remembered her aunt's terrible words. *What if Annika really believes she'd be second best?*

Now and then Pa slipped away on a short run to a nearby port. Always he hurried right back. In those times Libby, Caleb, and Gran stayed with the riverboat captain for whom Jordan's family worked.

One day when Pa was gone, Libby was at the hospital when Peter took a sudden turn for the worse. Seeing the doctor and nurses hurry in and out of the room shook Libby as deeply as that moment on the bluff.

With that strong sense of taking care of himself that he always had, Peter knew he was in trouble. Yet he was the one who comforted Libby. "I'm so tired, Libby," he said. "But I like having you here."

Slate in hand, she stayed by his bed, ready to talk whenever he opened his eyes.

"Wellington?" Peter asked one of those times. "You really are taking care of him?"

Libby nodded. "But he misses you."

"Where's Pa?" Peter wanted to know. Not *your* pa, but *Pa*, for Peter had begun calling him that.

"He'll be back tonight," Libby said. "Maybe even by supper. He tries to not leave at all. He thought you were doing better."

"If I die before he comes, will you say good-bye to him?"

Quick tears welled up in Libby's eyes. Holding her finger in front of her lips, she shook her head to tell him, "Don't say that!"

But Peter went on. "Pa is my father now, but my first papa and mama are in heaven. If I die, I'll go home to them. I'll see them again."

Suddenly Libby could handle no more. "Don't talk that way!" she wrote on the slate. "I can't stand it! You are going to live!"

Leaving the slate on the bed, Libby fled from the room. Going out on the wide porch on the upper floor, Libby looked toward the Galena River and began to pray. "Oh, God, what can I do? Peter is tired of fighting. He's giving up. How can I give him hope?"

In that still small voice that Libby was learning to recognize, she heard the answer: *Get Wellington.*

17

Where's Annika?

Off the porch, through the hall, down the steps to the bridge across the river Libby ran. Partway up the steep hill on the other side, she had to stop. When she caught her breath, she hurried on again.

At the captain's house, she found a large basket and two towels and hurried back outside. The terrier leaped up, trying to get her attention.

"C'mon, Wellington," she said. "We're going to see Peter."

The little dog seemed to understand, for his spindly legs churned along beside her. Back across the river they went, up the hill on that side. Behind a tree outside the hospital Libby stopped.

Putting down the basket, she lined it with one towel, then set Wellington inside. "You have to be quiet." Gently she pushed his back so he lay down. The dog whimpered.

"Be quiet, Wellington, or you won't see Peter," Libby said in her sternest voice.

The dog buried his muzzle between his paws. Libby put the second towel over him. "Quiet now. Be very quiet."

Carrying the basket, Libby set out again. Up the steps, through the hallways, up the stairs to the second floor she hurried. For the first time in his life, Wellington did not make a sound.

At Peter's room Libby stepped inside and closed the door. One look told her that Peter's eyes were closed. His face was so still and white that Libby wondered if he had died.

Then Wellington poked his head from under the towel. Suddenly he leaped from the basket onto the bed. When he nudged Peter with his nose, the boy's eyes flew open.

Gathering the dog in his arms, Peter hugged him. As though Wellington understood how sick Peter was, he wiggled once, then lay still.

From that moment on, Peter started getting well. When Pa visited Peter two hours later, he saw the difference. He also held up a piece of paper for Peter to read.

"My adoption?" Peter asked, his voice filled with awe. "I'm really your boy?"

Pa signed the words. "You're really my boy."

Peter looked at Libby. "And you're really my sister."

In the second week of November, Peter was well enough to leave the hospital. As the *Christina* headed upriver again, Pa's face was eager, his eyes lit with the hope of seeing Annika.

On this trip to St. Paul, Jordan's family went along. Jordan took all of them up to Pa's cabin and proudly showed them everything. "This is where I started learnin' to read and write!"

Jordan's momma and daddy looked around the room as if it was filled with glory.

After they left, Jordan's sister Serena and his brother, Zack, sat on the top deck with all the others. Leaning back against the wall of the texas, they let the sun beat down on them and watched the shoreline slide past.

Listening to them talk, Libby wondered if the others felt the way she did. *I don't want to say good-bye.*

During Peter's time in the hospital, Serena had become the friend Libby hoped for. More than once they had giggled together, sharing their secrets. In the most frightening moments of Peter's illness, Serena had offered encouragement. Libby hoped that she, too, had been a good friend to Serena.

At first the sun felt warm in spite of the lateness of the year. Peter still looked pale. But he sat with them, and his smile was stronger than ever. These days he always held Wellington in his arms. Usually the dog was content to stay there.

The farther north they traveled, the colder it became. All of them needed to take refuge in Pa's cabin. Serena wanted to see everything and spent most of her time at the windows. During their second night, the *Christina* passed through Lake Pepin, the widening in the Mississippi River.

Shortly after sunrise on their last morning together, Caleb called them to the railing. "Pan ice," he said, pointing at the river.

The ice looked like giant lily pads floating downstream. Roughly circular, each piece had a lacy fringe around the edge. The ice had a fragile look, as if it had just formed.

"It's beautiful!" Libby exclaimed.

Caleb didn't think so. "It's a bad sign. A sign of things to come. So far the ice isn't dangerous. See how the *Christina* plows through?"

From where she stood, Libby could see the thin ice breaking along the side of the bow. The fast-moving current swept away whatever pieces remained.

Libby didn't need Caleb to tell her that the ice would get worse. Instead he said, "Your pa wants to stay in St. Paul until he finds Annika. I don't think he'll get the chance."

"Oh, Caleb, don't say that."

Caleb was serious. "We better think of everything we can do to find Annika fast. If we don't, your pa isn't going to see her."

In spite of their warm coats, they soon needed to go back inside Pa's cabin. There Jordan looked around again, as if for the last time. His glance took in Libby and Caleb. "Remember how you started teachin' me to read?"

"Let's not say good-bye yet," Caleb said quickly. He, too, seemed to dread the farewell with Jordan. Over the months the boys had become best friends.

"We'll see Annika soon," Libby said in the silence that followed. The rest of the way to St. Paul, that thought held her. But then Jordan and his family, Libby, Caleb, Pa, and Peter gathered on the main deck.

"If you go somewhere else, be sure to leave word at the Winslow House," Pa told Jordan's father as he clapped him on the shoulder. "When we're back in town, we'll look you up."

As Jordan reached out for a handshake, Pa put an arm around his shoulder instead. Then Caleb and Peter said good-bye, and Jordan turned to say, "Thanks for everything, Libby."

Libby's good-bye to Serena was hardest of all. Her shining eyes and quiet smile reminded Libby how much she was losing.

"Thanks for being my friend," Libby told Serena. "See you next spring." She didn't want to admit this could be a final good-bye.

Then Micah Parker and his wife, Hattie, their sons, Jordan and Zack, and their daughters, Serena and Rose, walked down the gangplank into their new life.

"I'll miss Jordan and his family," Peter said. "I wonder how they'll get along."

"They'll be all right," Caleb signed, then wrote on the slate. "They'll find work and the church at St. Anthony." But Caleb looked even more upset than Peter to see Jordan leave.

When Peter and Pa left, Libby stayed near the gangplank, watching the Parker family start up Jackson Street. "It hurts to love people, doesn't it?"

"Sometimes," Caleb said.

"Like now?" Libby asked, thinking about how much Jordan meant to Caleb.

"Like now. And if someone you like doesn't pay much attention." Caleb glanced sideways at Libby as though telling her something he was afraid to say directly.

Libby looked up at him. To her surprise she really was looking up. In the past few months, Caleb had grown at least two inches and she hadn't even noticed.

"I'm sorry, Caleb," Libby said, then felt at a loss for words. *How can I tell him what he really means to me?* Just trying to think of the words was hard. But it seemed Caleb wanted to know.

"Being friends is helping each other," Libby said. "You've done that a lot for me."

And I usually objected, she told herself. *Most often I've thought Caleb was just doing what Pa asked him to do—watching out for me.*

"When I grow up—" Caleb started, and it sounded funny—as if he were still a little boy.

Caleb grinned, and the awkwardness between them vanished. "When I'm older, I'll be able to say all the things I think. Especially the things I think about you."

Libby giggled. As much as she liked Caleb, she felt relieved that it was more comfortable to talk with him again.

Then Caleb turned serious. "Friends talk about things that are important to them," he said. "Is that scary to you, Libby?"

"It's scary to me, Caleb. But if that's what it means to be a friend, I'll practice."

The minute that Pa could leave, he was off to find Annika. As Libby watched him hurry down the gangplank, Caleb said, "The music store isn't far from here. Let's see if Franz is still there."

Though it appeared that the economic panic had robbed the store of business, its doors were still open. Inside they found Franz. They soon learned that he had not recovered his stolen violin.

"I want to write to my family," Franz said. "I want to tell them my plans. But I need to find my fiddle first."

Because of the bad weather, Libby and Caleb could not stay long. On the way back to the *Christina*, they talked about the violin.

"Why hasn't someone found it in all this time?" Libby asked. "Does that mean it's gone forever? Taken someplace where Franz will never see it again?"

The idea bothered Libby. If that were true, it would be no use to continue searching. For Libby, doing nothing was the worst choice of all.

A few minutes after she and Caleb reached the *Christina*, Pa came up the gangplank.

"Annika isn't at the place where she was staying. The woman of the house said Annika moved out the end of September."

The south wind had a bite in it, but Pa stood on the deck with an open coat and no hat. Now he ran his fingers through his hair. "It's like we thought, Libby. Remember how both of us knew that something was wrong?"

Her heart in her throat, Libby nodded.

Pa shook his head as though unable to believe the bad news. "The woman said Annika found a temporary place, but then moved on from there. That's all she knew. I went to the school where Annika taught. She lost her job, and no one can tell me what happened to her. She just dropped out of sight."

As if suddenly realizing how cold it had become, Pa shivered. "Because of all the speculation, St. Paul was hit especially hard by the panic. There's little work and even less money. People say the city emptied out almost overnight. If Annika isn't teaching, what is she doing? Does she have enough food? Is she staying warm?"

Again Pa shivered and for the first time seemed to realize his coat was open. As he buttoned it, the captain from a nearby steamboat called to him. "Heading out soon?"

"Maybe."

"Temperature's dropping fast. If Pepin closes, we'll be locked in here all winter."

Pa nodded, though Libby doubted he heard. Instead, he glanced toward the men loading freight. The return trip would be light, Libby knew. There were also few passengers. Most of the people heading south had left long before.

For a moment Pa's gaze lingered on the nearly empty waterfront. When he looked back to Libby, pain filled his eyes. "I can't leave without knowing what's happened to Annika."

18

Ice Storm

"*Let's* give it two hours," Pa said. "Let's search as much as we can."

"I'll go to the *Pioneer and Democrat* office," Caleb offered. "People at a newspaper know what's going on. I'll stop at the police station too."

"I'll find Miss Bishop," Libby said just as quickly. As Peter joined them, she signed Annika's name.

"I'll ask at the stores and warehouses closest to the river," Peter answered.

"And I'll go to every hotel and boardinghouse within walking distance." Pa's voice was quiet but strong. Libby knew he was forcing himself to stay in control. This time he remembered to put on his captain's hat. But he still wore no gloves, as if nothing mattered but Annika.

Just watching him, Libby grieved. *The pain in Pa's heart matches the pain in his eyes.*

With her hurt for Pa growing by the minute, Libby set out to find Miss Bishop. When Libby reached the house, she knocked several times. Finally the lady next door came out to talk.

"You're looking for Harriet? She's been gone since early September. Can't tell you where. She wrote a book, you know.

Maybe she's traveling, talking to people about St. Paul."

Libby groaned. Her feet dragging, she headed back to the boat.

The rain started as a mist so fine that at first Libby thought she was seeing things. By the time she walked up the gangplank, her coat felt heavy with water. The wind still came from the south, but Libby had no doubt that in Minnesota Territory a November rain would soon mean ice.

Caleb was the next one to return, then Peter, and finally Pa. Long before the two hours were up, they gathered around the wood stove in the main cabin. All of them stretched out their hands toward the stove, but the heat did little to warm their hearts. Not one of them had learned anything about Annika.

Libby knew there was nothing more to say. The look in her father's face shook Libby to the center of her being.

Soon the chief engineer came into the cabin. "The temperature dropped ten degrees in the last hour. If we don't go now, we'll be here for the winter."

Having no choice but to leave St. Paul, Pa straightened his shoulders. "We'll leave the minute you're ready."

When the engineer hurried out, Pa turned to Libby and the boys. As though forcing himself to remember what was needed, he looked at each of them. "Thank you, Peter," he signed.

Peter wrapped his arms around Pa's waist and hugged him. As Pa stretched out his hand, Caleb put his own hand over Pa's. When her father's arm went around Libby's shoulder, she gave him the tightest hug she could. Then he hurried away, and Libby knew he wanted to be alone.

Going outside, she sat down on the wide steps at the front of the boat. Soon deckhands took in the lines, and the *Christina* slipped out into the river.

Libby stared at the black waters of the Mississippi. Her long wool stockings and her warmest coat, scarf, and mittens did little good today. The cold crept into her bones. Yet the ache she felt inside was worse.

Once again she watched the pan ice floating down the river. The giant lily pads seemed larger now. Crossing her arms, Libby hugged herself, but she could not keep away her fear. *Where is Annika?*

In answer to her question, Libby again remembered the verse Pa gave them the day Annika visited their class. With all her heart Libby tried to believe the words her mother had written in her Bible. Instead, Libby cried out in her spirit. *All things, God? How can you possibly bring something good out of something this awful?*

The cold rain slanted at an angle now, reaching under the overhang of the deck above. Libby felt glad there were no immigrants there, no children trying to stay warm. The empty deck made her lonesome for past friends—the runaway slave Emma and her baby, little Henry. The German immigrant Elsa. Jordan and his sister Serena. And now Annika.

Most of all, Libby's heart ached for Pa. With her hurt for him came more anger toward God. *How could you let Annika get lost? How can you be a good God, a kind God, when you treat Pa this way?*

Libby was shaking with cold when Caleb found her there. "Come inside where it's warm," he said. He led her to the large main cabin. As Libby huddled close to the stove, he asked, "What's really bothering you, Libby?"

As always, Libby felt afraid to talk. Then she remembered her promise to Caleb. *Friends tell each other the things that are important to them.*

"It's all my fault!" Libby wailed.

"What's your fault?"

"That Annika is lost, that Pa had to leave without seeing her." Starting with the words she had overheard in August, Libby explained. "Annika told Pa that I wasn't ready for a mother. She said if she came on board now, it would seem as if I snapped my fingers and *poof*! Like magic I had a mother."

When Libby finished talking, Caleb's eyes had that teasing look Libby knew too well. "Maybe Annika was right. Maybe there's a few things you need to change. Like hiding around a corner listening to your pa and Annika."

"But I *can't* change that now!" Caleb's words upset Libby even more. "What if Pa *never* has the chance to get things straightened out? How can I live the rest of my life knowing that he lost Annika because of me?"

"Because of *you*?" Caleb asked. "Who do you think you are, God or something?"

Lifting her head, Libby tossed her curls. "Of course I don't think I'm God!"

Caleb's voice changed, as if he really wanted to help. "Maybe you *weren't* ready for a new mother then. But you didn't cause the storm. And you didn't get Annika lost!"

Libby stared at him. "You said maybe I wasn't ready for a mother *then*. Does that mean I'm ready for a mother *now*?"

Caleb shrugged. "Maybe."

Maybe. Libby rolled the word around in her mind, then in her heart. *Caleb said maybe.*

Caleb leaned forward. "Libby, wherever Annika is, God is with her."

With his words the weight Libby had carried since August dropped from her. For the first time all day, she felt warm with hope. Her angry questions changed to a prayer letting God in. *Won't you help us? Please, won't you help us?*

As the *Christina* continued downriver, Pa called them together for school. When they gathered around the table in his cabin, Libby studied her father's face. *He needs something to think about besides Annika.*

In the small upper room it was growing colder all the time. Libby's breath hung in the frosty air. Whenever she turned a page, she needed to take off her mitten.

Like the rest of them, Pa wore his warmest jacket, gloves, and scarf. He looked exhausted, something Libby never saw. He seemed to be walking in his sleep.

Pa had barely begun teaching when the wind rattled the windows. Like a spray of small stones, bits of ice struck the glass. In that moment Libby heard the change. The rain had turned to sleet, pelting the glass. But the sleet also brought Pa back to his usual self.

"We'll have to make a run for it," he said as calmly as if he faced an ice-bound Lake Pepin every day. "Take your books down to the main cabin. Push a table closer to the stove. It's too cold for you here."

When Libby stepped out on deck, the wind had swung around, coming from the northwest. Soon after they passed Red Wing, the Mississippi River widened into a lake twenty-two miles long and one to three miles wide. Because the current was slower, Lake Pepin always froze sooner than the river above or below it.

Behind the boat the river looked choppy, as troubled as Libby felt about their trip through the lake. Closer to shore and ahead of the *Christina*, the water was smooth, even glasslike. That look of glass told Libby the water was freezing.

Pushing aside her dread, she went into the large cabin. At first she managed to study. Then Libby began seeing water instead of pages filled with numbers. Though she tried hard, she couldn't shut out the frightening pictures that passed through her mind.

Closing her eyes, she tried to forget the boat she had seen last spring. Thrown by wind and ice against Pepin's shore, the steamboat had leaned sideways and filled with water as passengers scrambled to get off.

Finally Libby put on her coat and wound a long scarf around her head and neck. Stepping outside again, she stood at the railing. The sleet had stopped now, but a half-inch layer of ice had formed over the surface of Lake Pepin. As Caleb came to stand beside her, Libby asked, "It's closing in, isn't it?"

Caleb nodded as though not wanting to admit the truth.

"What if the ice catches us?"

"Don't ask," he said. "You won't want to know."

Then Libby remembered. Caleb had been with Pa last winter when the *Christina* was caught by unseasonable ice farther downriver. Pa seldom spoke about that time. Libby only knew that he had to have the hull rebuilt.

"This is only November thirteenth! People in St. Paul said that if the river closes, it's the earliest on record."

Libby's words made Caleb impatient. "Records don't count," he said, sounding more upset than he wanted to admit. "What counts is whether we get through safely."

Standing there, Libby wondered if the ice had grown thicker even as they spoke. As she watched, the ship's carpenter crept out on the forward deck. At the starboard, or right, side of the boat, he dropped onto his stomach. There he looked down over the guards, the boards that extended out over the hull.

"What's he doing?" Libby asked.

"Checking for ice damage."

A moment later the carpenter checked the port, or left, side of the boat and called to a deckhand. "It's taking her paint!"

Libby's stomach tightened. Like a young child, she wanted to be with her father. "Let's go up to the pilothouse."

On the side deck, sleet had coated the boards, making them slick. "Hang on," Caleb warned as they started up the stairs.

Libby wrapped her mittens around the ice-coated railing as if her life depended on it. On the hurricane deck, she felt the full blast of the cold wind. There in the open, the ice was so slippery that Caleb dropped to his hands and knees. Libby followed him, crawling across the deck.

One after the other, they crept up the stairs to the pilothouse. Caleb opened the door with glass in the top half, and hung on with all his strength. While Libby crawled inside, he held the door against the draft, then closed it without breaking the glass.

Fletcher, the pilot, stood at the side of the great wheel with Pa next to him. Besides being owner of the *Christina*, Pa was also licensed as a pilot, but he helped only as needed. His quick smile welcomed Libby and Caleb. Then he turned once more to lock his gaze onto the lake ahead.

On the front side of the pilothouse, the hinged boards at the top and bottom of the opening were nearly closed against the weather. Pa and Fletcher peered through the narrow opening that remained. Glass windows filled the other three walls, but one whole side had iced over. Minute by minute, conditions were growing worse.

As Libby looked around, she saw the far shore of Lake Pepin along the eastern horizon. On the west and closer side, the land was stripped bare of trees, but not of rocks. Behind the *Christina* a narrow trail of black water showed where the boat had passed through, breaking the ice. Ahead, and growing thicker by the hour, the ice stretched out as far as Libby could see.

Soon a deckhand came to the door. Holding it open long enough to talk to Pa, he said, "Carpenter says the ice is splintering the hull."

Within minutes another crew member opened the door. "Engineer says there's ice in the buckets."

"What's he talking about?" Libby whispered to Caleb.

"The wood planks on the paddle wheels. The buckets catch the water and send the boat forward."

"And they're plugging up with ice?"

"Carrying too heavy a load."

Pa turned to Libby. "If the ice breaks the paddle wheels, we can't move ahead, no matter how hard we try. We'll freeze into the lake."

Libby swallowed hard. In her wildest imagination, she hadn't thought of something that terrible. The *Christina* frozen all winter in the great open stretches of Lake Pepin?

Yet there was something even worse. In the spring breakup, the *Christina* would have no protection. Caught by tons of floating ice, the boat would be thrown up on shore like matchsticks!

19

Swede Hollow

Fletcher stepped aside to let Pa take the wheel. Leaning forward, Pa spoke down the tube into the engine room. "All hands prepare to back out."

A moment later he called down the next order. "Reverse wheels."

As the engines stopped, Libby felt the wind from behind push them against the ice. Almost at once, the paddle wheels reversed, and the engines started again. Yet in that brief time the wind and current had pushed the ice in the channel against the *Christina*'s stern.

Libby glanced at Caleb, not daring to speak. Caleb leaned close.

"The rudder," he whispered, and Libby knew she had reason to be afraid.

The shaft of the rudder projected out back of the stern and down into the water. That stock held the rudder, a large board shaped like a capital D that steered the *Christina*.

"What if the rudder breaks?" Libby whispered back.

Behind the *Christina* the open channel was only the width of the boat. With his hand on the large wheel, Pa stood sideways, looking upriver as he backed the steamboat through the narrow trail the boat had opened. With each turn of the paddle wheels, the *Christina* pushed into the ice lodged against her rudder.

At first that ice was like a wall against the *Christina*'s stern. For a quarter of a mile Pa backed, slowly, gingerly, trying to get free of the ice that had piled up in the minute they stopped. When the last chunks fell away, Libby breathed deep. But her relief lasted only a moment.

Soon the *Christina* veered off. Leaving the trail of open water, she swung into the unbroken mass of ice on one side.

The door to the pilothouse opened. "Chief engineer says we've lost our rudder."

"On your toes," Pa answered as if expecting this. "We'll steer with the wheels, but first we have to turn."

Again Libby looked at Caleb, then at the wooden housing that surrounded the paddle wheels above the water line. Each of those wheels was operated by its own engine, independent of the other. While the chief engineer operated one wheel, the assistant engineer took the controls on the other. By reversing one wheel and going forward with the other, the *Christina* would turn. Yet what could be simple under ordinary conditions had become extremely dangerous.

This time even Caleb looked afraid. Fletcher's worried look matched Pa's.

With dread Libby remembered her father's words. Not having a rudder was bad enough. If the ice broke a paddle wheel, the *Christina* would go around in circles. Now Libby wondered how they could possibly turn without the ice backing up along one side. The pressure against the wood housing and the paddle wheel could splinter them into thousands of pieces.

In spite of the cold, beads of sweat stood out on Pa's forehead. For one instant he closed his eyes, gritting his teeth. "Everyone pray for a miracle," he said, then leaned forward and spoke into the tube.

"Prepare to turn. I'll give a rapid series of orders. Respond as quickly as you can."

His commands clear and strong, Pa spoke without hesitation. "Come ahead easy on the starboard wheel. Come back easy on the port."

As the *Christina* responded, she edged out from the solid mass of ice next to the open water. "Stop your port wheel. Come back strong on the port wheel."

Libby held her breath.

"Stop your starboard wheel," Pa ordered. "Stop your port wheel. Come back strong on the port wheel."

In the next moment the *Christina*'s bow turned upstream. As the backed-up ice slid off the housing around the paddle wheel, Libby breathed deep with relief.

"Hold her there," Pa called down. "You're in open water. Hold her steady."

A moment later he turned to Libby and Caleb. "We seem to have our miracle!"

Suddenly it struck Libby what that meant. Filled with excitement, she led Caleb from the pilothouse. Across the icy deck they inched. But when they reached the large main cabin where Pa could not hear, Libby raised her arms in victory. "We're going back! We're going back to St. Paul!"

Caleb grinned. "Now all we have to do is find Annika!"

"And the stolen violin! Why haven't we found it in all this time? Why hasn't Franz found it?"

Then Libby had a dreadful thought. "What if the violin has been taken down the Mississippi to New Orleans? Or across America on one of the trains to New York? By now the violin could be in Europe!"

For at least ten miles, the *Christina* followed the narrow channel of open water she had opened coming down. After what seemed forever, the steamboat passed out of Lake Pepin.

In the swiftly flowing water of the Mississippi's main channel, there was less ice. Yet they could waste no time in reaching a winter harbor. At a safe place, the *Christina* pulled over to one side of the river. The ship's carpenter attached a makeshift rudder that would work until better repairs could be made.

As they drew close to St. Paul, Libby heard Pa humming. When he caught her eye, Pa laughed. "Maybe there was a reason why Annika thought she should stay in St. Paul this winter."

The early November darkness had already settled over the river as Pa and his crew began looking for a safe harbor in the backwaters. A short distance below St. Paul, they found an island big enough to protect the *Christina* from what could be a thirty-foot pile of ice in spring. Fletcher guided the steamboat into her winter home.

As Libby stood at the bow of the *Christina*, a high bluff rose from the starboard side. Across the island and upstream lay the bluffs on which St. Paul was built. By daylight they would be able to see the homes, businesses, and tall church spires.

The minute the lines were out, deckhands with rooms on the texas began moving down to staterooms usually used by first-class passengers. Pa assigned the staterooms closest to the wood stove to Gran and Libby. Then he and the crew members who chose to stay on board took rooms nearby. That night the ice in the backwaters froze around the *Christina's* hull.

The next morning Pa walked into St. Paul. He returned with a horse-drawn wagon filled with lumber. Together he and his men boarded off the end of the cabin that had the wood stove. Instead of one long, narrow room that would take mountains of wood to heat, they now had a room large enough for the few people left on board to sit around, talk, and eat.

As soon as the new wall was built, Pa set his men to hauling firewood for the long winter ahead. Then Pa returned to St. Paul to begin his search for Annika.

After he left, Libby looked around the room Pa had created in the main cabin. The new wall was made of rough sawn wood, the only thing available in this town where the need for houses had been so great. The wall looked completely different from anything else in the large, elegant room that Libby had always loved. Yet staying warm was more important than having a smoothly painted wall.

Standing in their new winter room, Libby remembered the immigrant family that had stretched a piece of canvas between two barrels to make a roof. She thought about the tepees of the oxcart drivers and the way they draped hides over their carts. *They all made a shelter—a home—wherever they were.*

Wearing her warmest coat, Libby walked into the part of the cabin that had been shut off. The chairs and tables stood as they always had but now looked strangely deserted. It was the paintings Libby came to see—the large paintings centered on white panels along the walls.

Walking up and down the long room, Libby chose the three she liked best. From the carpenter's supply she found a hammer, nails, and a small ladder. Working together, she and Peter took down the paintings and hung them on the new wooden wall. Together they carried Pa's big rocking chair from his cabin on the texas.

When Pa returned late in the day, it was already dark. Libby took one look at his face and knew he had found no trace of Annika. Then Pa saw his rocking chair and the paintings.

At the center of the wall, a north woods scene showed farmland, hills, and trees surrounding a small house. From the bluff there was a view of the river.

Pa stopped in front of the painting. "You did this, didn't you?" he asked Libby.

"With Peter's help."

"You're growing up," Pa said gently. "You're learning how to make a home."

His voice was gruff, and he turned away quickly, but Libby saw the tears in his eyes. "I'd still like to see the land you bought," she told him.

"Sometime, Libby," Pa promised. "Not now."

The next morning Caleb and the crew hauled wood, and Pa walked into St. Paul again. This time Libby went with him. Near the Lower Landing, Pa went one way and Libby another.

She asked questions wherever she could, hoping to learn something about Annika that Pa hadn't.

At last she gave up looking for the teacher and walked to the music store.

Franz was surprised to see her. "I thought you left."

"We did," Libby said. "We had to come back."

"But you're all right now?" Franz asked when he heard the story.

"Except for Annika. She stayed in St. Paul, and we can't find her."

"Ach!" Franz exclaimed. "In my country—" Suddenly he broke off, as if he had said more than he intended. "Is there a way I can help you find Annika?"

Libby felt glad for anyone who would help. "Listen," she said. "Ask questions whenever you can."

"I want to find my relatives the way you want to find your Annika," Franz said.

"Your relatives?" Franz had not mentioned them before.

"My cousin and his family. I wish to talk to him. To see how he does, living on a farm near the village called Nicollet."

"Where's Nicollet?" Libby asked.

"South and west of here in Minnesota Territory. Between St. Peter and New Ulm. But I cannot leave until I find my violin."

"We still want to do whatever we can to help," Libby promised.

All the way back to the *Christina*, Libby thought about her promise to Franz. The minute she reached home, Libby found Peter. Taking his slate, she wrote *Suspects*, then listed the three men:

1. *tall Shadowman*
2. *short pawnbroker*
3. *tall Mr. Trouble*

"But which tall man has a violin mark below his jawline?" Libby asked. "And who is Shadowman?"

While Pa searched for Annika, Peter taught Wellington more commands. He wanted the dog to find Libby even if he couldn't see her.

"Let's play hide-and-seek," Peter told Libby as they walked along the main deck. "I'll throw a stick so Wellington doesn't see where you're going. I'll use my secret sign to send him after you."

The moment Peter threw the stick, Wellington raced down the deck. Libby slipped inside the engine room and left the door behind her slightly open. She found a hiding place behind a big piece of equipment.

Soon she heard Wellington sniffing his way toward her. When the terrier found her, Libby hugged him and slipped him a treat. "Good dog! Good dog!"

Peter's eyes shone. Again and again he asked Libby to hide. He wanted to be sure Wellington remembered the secret sign.

If only we could have Wellington find Annika, Libby thought.

Each day Pa, Libby, Caleb, Peter, and Gran had prayed together for Annika. On the third morning after returning to St. Paul, they again gathered around the breakfast table. Pa needed to talk.

"Annika was so sure God wanted her in St. Paul this winter," he said. "Because she believed that, I don't think she'd leave. She has to be here. But if she is, why can't we find her?"

Not even Gran had an answer, and Pa went on. "My greatest dread is that something happened to her. If she became sick, we wouldn't even know who took care of her."

After they once again prayed for Annika, Caleb spoke up. "I'd like to go into St. Paul with you today."

Pa looked grateful. "Thanks, Caleb. I could use your help."

When they returned home that evening, Caleb looked so excited that Libby thought they had found Annika. But he only said, "I got work at the *Pioneer and Democrat* office today."

"The St. Paul newspaper?"

"One of them."

"Really? They took you on as a writer?"

"Oh no!" Caleb exclaimed. "In these hard times I couldn't possibly get a job as a reporter. Besides, people think I'm too young. But I did get a job emptying trash and sweeping floors one or two hours a day."

Libby felt curious. "How is that going to help you be a better writer?"

Caleb grinned. "I'll get in on the ground floor."

Then he grew serious. "As I sweep floors I'll listen. I'll see what reporters and editors are doing. I'll learn from them. Maybe sometime I'll get the chance to write something."

Later Libby and Caleb went out on deck, and Caleb said more. "What your pa is trying to do is really hard, you know. Thousands of immigrants passed through St. Paul this summer."

"It scares me, Caleb," Libby said.

"At the beginning of the panic, there must have been ten thousand people in the city. Unless someone stays with a group of people who know each other well, a person like Annika can drop out of sight."

Right down to her toes Libby felt frightened just thinking about Pa's loss. "Isn't there *anything* you remember about her that would help?"

For a moment Caleb was silent, thinking about it. "Swedish!" he said suddenly. "Annika is Swedish!"

"But Annika has black hair." She certainly didn't look Swedish to Libby.

"Just the same, she is!" Caleb exclaimed. "We talked about it once. One of her ancestors was a Walloon from the French-speaking part of Belgium."

He explained that the Walloons came from southern Belgium. They were skilled ironworkers and blacksmiths and miners. When the leader of the Swedish iron industries asked for their help, several hundred emigrated to Sweden. They played an important part in Sweden's industrial growth.

Already Caleb's mind was running ahead. "I just need to find a settlement of Swedes."

Libby knew that when people came to America, they often settled with people who knew the same language. It helped them during the time when they were learning English.

"I'll ask at the *Pioneer* office," Caleb said. "I'll find out where the Swedes are."

When Caleb returned that night, he was even more excited. He led Libby out on the deck where they could talk without anyone else hearing. "I don't want to raise your pa's hopes until I know. Tomorrow you and Peter and I are going to *Svenska Dalen*."

"Svenska Dalen?"

"Swedish Valley. Most people call it Swede Hollow."

Then Caleb said, "Libby, there's something else. The reporters were talking about a man who's a big, well-known crook. The police think he came to St. Paul to hide from the law. Tall. Brown hair. Blue eyes. A cruel mouth."

Filled with dread, Libby stared at Caleb. "Mr. Trouble?"

"I think so. He fits the description."

"Then he's the brains behind everything?"

"I don't know," Caleb said. "But it would help the police to see your drawing."

20

Samson Again

During the night it snowed again. In the morning Caleb decided that Peter needed more time to get well before walking all the way to Swede Hollow. As Libby and Caleb set out, she looked back and saw the tracks they had made up the steep hill next to the backwaters. The tall white steamboat looked like an ice palace surrounded by snow.

On the way there, Caleb told Libby more about Swede Hollow. "It's a ravine—a narrow place between steep bluffs. Fur traders lived in the ravine for a while. When they moved on, Swedish immigrants moved in. They started fixing up the houses—"

Caleb corrected himself. "Shacks, the men at the newspaper called them. People stay in the shacks by paying the city five dollars a month for taxes. It's a hidden-away part of St. Paul. If Annika is there, it's no wonder your pa can't find her."

Before long they came to the edge of the ravine. Looking down, Caleb whistled. "It's seventy feet deep!"

The sides of the ravine were nearly straight up and down. At the bottom of the valley was a swiftly moving stream that Caleb called Phalen Creek. Even from where Libby stood, she heard the water rippling over the stones.

Stilts supported the front side of each house, while the back side was built into the bluff. The houses were small and hastily put up, but to Libby the size didn't matter. There was something about them that she liked.

What is it? she wondered, puzzled by what she felt.

In Chicago she had lived with Aunt Vi in a mansion, but Libby couldn't call these buildings shacks. Many of the houses showed repair. More than once a front porch or a room had been added. In the steep sides of the ravine, people had set large wooden tubs for flowers to grow in the summer.

Libby struggled to put what she was feeling into words. Then she knew what it was. *A sense of caring. They've taken what they have and made the best of it.*

A new dusting of snow lay over the tucked-away village, making everything clean. As though she could see inside the small houses, Libby imagined family and friends meeting over a cup of coffee. Gathering around a wood stove to talk in the language they knew. Living in a valley that reminded them of the country they left.

If Annika is here, she's made a home.

At an open spot between trees, Caleb crouched low. "I'll show you the quickest way down," he said. On the steep side of the ravine, his boots slid forward. Stretching out his arms, he swooped downward. A trail of snow fanned out behind him.

A short distance from the creek, he leaned over and sprawled in a bank of snow. "C'mon! It's great!" he called.

Libby gulped, just looking at Caleb far below.

"You can do it!" he shouted. "But don't hit a tree! Roll on your side if you need to stop!"

The moment Libby crouched down, she felt herself slide forward. With her slippery shoes, it worked! Then she looked to the bottom of the ravine and panicked, lost her balance, and tumbled into the snow. When she picked herself up, she crouched low again.

This time she dragged her hands behind her, ready to stop if needed. Faster and faster she went, swooping down the hill. Full of laughter, she landed in the soft snow at the bottom.

Libby and Caleb began their search by knocking on the nearest door to ask for Annika Berg. On their first try, a woman said, "Yah, sure, she teaches my children to read and write. She teaches them to love America."

The woman pointed to a house farther down the hollow. When Caleb knocked there, another woman opened the door. "Yah, yah, the teacher lives here. But she is gone now. Come back in an hour or two."

"We found her!" Libby exclaimed. "I can't believe it!" After all their searching, it seemed too good to be true.

While they waited, she and Caleb walked through the hollow. Soon they came to a wider path leading up and out of the ravine. As Libby looked ahead, she saw a young woman coming toward her. In the morning sunlight her black hair shone. The cold air brought out the color of her cheeks.

Libby broke into a run. "Annika!" she called. "We found you!"

In the middle of the path the teacher stopped. Then she, too, started running. As they met halfway, Annika threw her arms around Libby in a big hug.

When Annika stepped back, she cupped Libby's face in her hands. "Oh, Libby," she said, beginning to cry. "I didn't know if I'd ever see you again."

Now it was Libby who hugged her. When Annika finally stopped weeping, she asked one question. "Your pa?"

Libby grinned. "This is the fifth day he's climbed every hill in St. Paul looking for you."

She watched the teacher's face. "Annika, did you really mean to say good-bye to us? Good-bye forever?"

The teacher's deep blue eyes met Libby's. "I was very angry when I said that. Angry with your aunt Vi. My pride got in the way."

"Pa wasn't gone from the *Christina* the way Auntie said. We didn't find out about the note you gave her till we were far down the river. What she told you isn't true."

A red flush crept into Annika's cheeks. "About being second best?"

Libby nodded. "Pa doesn't want *anyone* to feel second best. Especially the woman he loves."

Startled, Annika blinked. Once again tears welled up in her eyes. She tried to brush them away.

"Pa would have telegraphed you from Galena," Libby said. "But the telegraph hasn't reached St. Paul. So he searched out a steamboat captain and sent a letter."

Tears streamed down Annika's cheeks. "I never received it. If you couldn't find me, the captain probably couldn't find me either."

As she wiped her cheeks, Annika drew a deep breath. Suddenly she remembered Caleb. When she tried to shake his hand, he hugged her instead. Then Annika led them to the house where she stayed. The first thing she did was cancel classes for the day.

Off to one side of the small house, a room had been added. Annika showed it to them. "See how well the Lord provided when my teaching position fell through?"

"What happened?" Libby asked.

"The panic," Annika began. "Everything changed. Hundreds of people left St. Paul. Banks closed. The little money there was had no value. If people had something to sell, they wanted gold. Harriet might have been able to help me, but she left soon after you did."

"Didn't you wonder if you had heard God wrong?" Libby asked. "About staying in St. Paul, I mean?"

Annika smiled. "It certainly crossed my mind. But when I asked for help, God led me here."

Annika's outstretched hand took in the small room. "The people of the hollow who had jobs took up a collection to buy lumber. The men who didn't have work built this room. When I said, 'It is too much, too much,' they told me, 'It is too much that you teach our children.' "

"Can you come with us for the day?" Libby asked. "We don't know how to find Pa. But if we go to the *Christina*, you'll be there when he comes home."

At the *Christina* Libby surprised Peter with the news. "Look who we found!" Together with Gran, they gathered around the wood stove to wait for Pa.

Several times that day, Libby went up to the hurricane deck to look toward St. Paul. Against the setting sun, she finally saw

Pa in the distance. He walked with dragging steps and slumped shoulders.

Libby raced down to the *Christina*'s winter room to find Annika. "Pa's coming!"

Annika snatched up her coat and hurried from the room. Down the stairs to the main deck she raced, then across the gangplank.

As Annika started up the hill, Pa suddenly stopped. Then he straightened for a better look. The next instant he started running.

Pa and Annika met on the side of the hill, and his arms went around her. As he bowed his head, his shoulders shook, and Libby knew he was weeping.

Then Libby remembered what Pa and Caleb had told her. Though it was one of the hardest things she had ever done, Libby turned around. She even walked away to give Pa and Annika time alone.

When at last they came inside, Libby had straightened up the *Christina*'s winter room. Caleb had made it cozy with wood heat. Gran had coffee and supper ready, and Peter held Wellington in his arms.

As they ate supper together, Annika sat next to Pa. "Day after day I walked to the Lower Landing and watched for the *Christina*," she told him. "But time passed, and you didn't come. Then the river froze—" Annika stopped, unable to go on.

"Did you think I had forgotten you?"

Annika shook her head. "I knew something was wrong. I feared the worst."

A smile lit her face. "Thank you for coming back."

Pa put his hand over hers. "Thank you for waiting for me."

Then Pa drew back. "You say you're living in Swede Hollow? Will those Swedes allow a Norwegian to court you?"

"Not if you tell them." Annika's eyes had that look of mischief again.

From that moment on, Pa showed Annika that he took their courtship seriously. Often he and Annika disappeared for sleigh rides and skating on the Mississippi River. In spite of her best attempts to behave and not listen in, Libby sometimes heard what they said. Once, it was about Peter.

"You adopted him?" Annika asked.

"I wanted to talk with you first," Pa said. "I didn't know how you felt, even about me. I believed you would want Peter to be part of our family. But I knew that even if you didn't—even if it became a reason why you wouldn't want to marry me—I still wanted to adopt Peter for his sake."

Annika looked into Pa's eyes. "Nathaniel, I love you for yourself. I love you for your caring heart. Often I've wondered, 'How will I know if I've found a man who will be a good father?' Seeing you with Libby and Peter, I know exactly the kind of father you are."

Annika blinked away her tears. "It would be my honor to be Libby's mother and Peter's too."

That night they made plans for Thanksgiving Day. "It's on December tenth this year," Annika reminded them.

"Let's invite Jordan's family," Caleb said.

Libby joined in. "And the fiddler too. He doesn't have a family here."

"Could we have our Thanksgiving on the *Christina*?" Annika asked Pa.

And so it was decided. On Thanksgiving morning Micah Parker would bring his family from St. Anthony in a sleigh. Jordan would come the day before so he could spend extra time with Caleb.

During the days that followed, Libby, Caleb, and Peter went back to work on finding the fiddler's violin.

When Annika asked about their search, she said, "Libby, you shouldn't walk about the streets of St. Paul alone. Remember the man who crept into your room? How he looked for the picture you drew? Remember the men who stole furs from the warehouse?"

Libby nodded. Those furs had never been found. With Annika's reminder, Libby's fear returned.

"You don't know who the men are, but they know you," Annika warned.

"They've probably left St. Paul by now." Libby tried to pretend that the men didn't scare her.

"But we don't know," Annika said. "We just don't know. If you go somewhere alone, why don't you take Samson along?"

21

Trapped!

"*S*hadowman," Caleb said as he wrote on the big blackboard from Pa's cabin. "Mr. Trouble. The pawnbroker."

Under the names Caleb wrote quickly for Peter, "What do we know about the thief who stole the fiddle?"

"The man in the music store said he has a red mark on his neck," Libby said.

"The oxcart driver thought the thief didn't really want to sell the violin," Caleb added.

"The first time we came to St. Paul, there were three men on the *Christina* we didn't trust," Libby said. "And three men stole the furs."

In a way that reminded Libby of Caleb, Peter brushed the blond hair out of his eyes. "I think the man who stole the violin finds whatever people he needs to help him."

"What do you mean?" Caleb signed.

"The thief is someone smart," Peter explained. "Sometimes he works on his own, like when he stole the violin. If he needs more men for something like stealing furs, he finds them."

Caleb clapped Peter on the back. "You've got it!" he wrote. "And we can be sure of one thing. The pawnbroker wanted to collect the reward on Jordan. More than likely, he talked to Riggs."

"So we've got either one thief or three." The idea frightened Libby. "If that's true, the thieves want to get money in whatever way they can."

Libby looked at Caleb. "You gave my drawing of Mr. Trouble to the police. They said he fits the description of a well-known crook—someone hiding from the law. Do you think Mr. Trouble is the leader in all this?"

Calen shrugged. "When they need a tough guy, he might do the mean stuff."

"But who's the brains?" Libby asked. "The one who plans everything? Could it be Shadowman?"

Caleb shrugged. "We're missing something important. Something so simple that it's right in front of us."

"We need to start over," Libby said as they finished talking.

During the night, she decided what to do. For Libby, starting over meant going back to the first place they looked. But she didn't want anyone else along. Already she was thinking about Christmas. If she was careful with the small amount of money she had, she could make drawings for everyone. On her way to the pawnshop she would buy art supplies.

The next morning Libby told the others she was going into town. When Caleb offered to go with her, she shook her head. Instead, she agreed to meet everyone at Annika's for a late afternoon meal.

When Libby was ready to leave, Samson followed her down to the gangplank. Libby commanded, "Stay!"

Samson dropped to his haunches. As he tipped his head and whined, Libby remembered Annika's warning about taking the dog along. Instead, Libby pushed the thought away. *Samson is such a pest. Besides, I won't be out after dark.*

After shutting the dog in, Libby set out. All the way into St. Paul, she thought about the stolen violin.

Libby soon found a general store that sold food and clothing, tools, and art supplies. The walls of the store were lined with shelves, but many of them were empty.

As Libby explained what she wanted, the storekeeper shook

his head. "I'm sorry. I ordered that kind of paper and those pencils, but the river closed so early that we didn't get our shipment."

Disappointed, Libby turned away, but the man called after her. "Have you tried using charcoal crayons? We have some left."

He held up what looked like a small black stick, then drew on a piece of paper. "See the heavy line it makes? Or you can do something soft and light."

Libby hadn't used charcoal, but now she had no choice but to learn. As the storekeeper wrapped her package, she saw Oliver White enter the store.

Turning quickly, Libby stood with her back to the man. She didn't want to talk with him about Annika and hoped he wouldn't see her.

Two days after finding the teacher, Libby had asked her about Mr. White.

"When I moved to Swede Hollow, I didn't tell him where I went," Annika had explained.

"He didn't find you? You never bumped into him on the street?"

Annika shook her head and smiled but said no more.

The moment Libby's package was ready, she hurried out of the store. By now it was the middle of the afternoon, and Libby headed for the pawnshop. When she reached it, she opened the door slowly so the jangling bell didn't ring.

The large room looked much the same as in August, except for one thing. Hard times had come, and the well-protected cases were filled to overflowing.

On the right side of the dimly lit room, both doors stood partway open. Through one doorway Libby saw a hall that led to the back of the building. From there she heard the voices of two men.

Libby stepped closer to the second door. Without making a sound, she pushed it open into a small closet with shelves from floor to ceiling. As Libby's eyes grew used to the darkness, she saw a man's gold watch and a costly necklace. Then Libby found it. *A violin case!*

Her heart pounding, she brought the case to the larger room. There where she could see, Libby lifted the cover. Picking up the violin, she turned it over.

In that instant the sound of voices in the back room changed. One of the men had moved closer.

Libby set the violin in its case, closed the cover, and leaped up. She quickly returned the case to the closet shelf. Returning to the larger room, she pulled the closet door partway shut behind her and hurried over to the wall of musical instruments.

"I didn't hear you come in," the man said as he entered the room. "Have you been here long?"

Libby drew a deep breath and turned to face him. Before her stood the short, thin pawnbroker who had threatened Jordan.

What if he remembers me? Libby thought, her heart pounding again.

She tried to speak calmly. "I'm looking for a violin for someone who plays well. Are these for sale?"

The man showed her three violins. Each time Libby took one, she looked it over and tried to play a note or two. Tucking the chin rest in place, she drew the bow across the strings. The screech sent shivers up her arm.

Libby forced herself to smile. "Good thing it's not for me."

Finally she said, "I'll talk to my father. If he's able to come today, how long are you open?"

When Libby turned toward the door, she nearly crashed into a man coming in. In the dim light of the pawnshop, his hat shadowed his face. Dressed for the cold, he wore a long black coat.

Then Libby realized who he was. Mr. Oliver White III! Inwardly she groaned. *I haven't seen him since August. Now two times in one day!*

A startled look crossed his face. His hand went to the brim of his hat as though to lift it. "Miss Norstad," he said. "I didn't realize you were in town."

"Mr. White," she answered just as politely. After avoiding him earlier, Libby had no choice but to talk with him now. "Are you living in St. Paul?"

The tall young man smiled. "I'm here for the winter. I've always been grateful to your father for introducing Miss Berg to me."

And I've always wished he hadn't, Libby thought. *Somehow you always show up at the wrong time.*

"Miss Berg is a splendid young woman." Mr. White sounded as if he had been seeing her every day.

"I'm sure she's a very good teacher," Libby said. Her thoughts tumbled on. *And I'm sure you want to know where Annika is. Well, I'm not going to be the one who tells you!*

"Are you finding what you need?" he asked.

Libby swallowed hard. "Yes, Mr. White," she said softly. "I found everything I need."

Outdoors once more, Libby took the street that ran along the side of the building. Sunshine had turned the snow to slush, and she walked quickly. She had almost reached the next corner when she turned around.

From here she could see the back wall of the pawnshop. Bars covered a door and two windows. A man stood at one of the windows, watching her.

Pretending that nothing was wrong, Libby turned and walked on. *Who is he?* she wondered. The bars on the window hid enough of the man's face so she wasn't sure.

As she headed for Swede Hollow, frightened thoughts filled her mind. *Did I put the fiddle on the right shelf and leave the door the way I found it? Did I hide my excitement?*

She had no way of being sure about anything. Her panic growing, Libby walked faster and faster. She was three blocks from the pawnshop when she heard a strange sound behind her.

Footsteps? No. The snow isn't cold enough for that. Telling herself that she was being foolish, Libby pushed aside her uneasiness. Then she remembered. *Slush. Would I hear someone walking in slush?*

Each time she glanced over her shoulder, she found nothing unusual and hurried on. Finally she felt so uneasy that she whirled around. In the split second before a man stepped out of sight, Libby saw his face. *The man I drew on the boat. The man whose picture I put in the* Christina's *safe. Mr. Trouble!*

Libby gulped. *The voices in the back room. So Peter was right! Mr. Trouble and the pawnbroker are working together!*

Libby broke into a run. *Why didn't I bring Samson along?*

Before long her side ached, and Libby knew she couldn't make it to Swede Hollow. More than that, she didn't want to lead Mr. Trouble to Annika's house.

By now she was back on the street where she had purchased her art supplies. The general store was a welcome sight. *I'll be safe there! But just in case, someone needs to know where I am.*

Close to the building was a line of snow where the sun didn't reach. Tearing open her package, Libby grabbed a piece of charcoal. By the time she reached the door she was ready. With one swift movement she reached down and drew a fish in the snow.

Once more she looked back. No one in sight. Libby ducked into the doorway. With a quick bound she was inside.

As she caught her breath, Libby looked around. The shopkeeper who helped her before was nowhere in sight. He had propped up a sign on the counter:

Please pick out what you need.
I'll return in fifteen minutes.

Trusting soul, Libby thought. *Maybe the people of St. Paul are so honest it doesn't matter.*

Then Libby realized something else. *There's no one here to protect me.*

Her heart in her throat, Libby looked through the large panes of glass at the front of the store. Just then she saw Mr. Trouble come into view.

Like a rabbit fleeing from Wellingon, Libby raced to the back of the room. Behind high shelves she stopped. A minute later the front door opened. Libby heard heavy footsteps crossing the store. Frantic now, she searched for a way to escape.

A door led to a back room. Libby turned the knob, and the door opened into total darkness. As far as Libby could tell, the room had no windows. Stepping inside, she left the door behind her cracked open to the light.

Closer and closer the footsteps came. *Is it Mr. Trouble?*

Next to the partly opened door, Libby pressed against the wall and looked into the other room. In the shadows away from the front windows, she saw a movement. Then she heard the scratch of a match. A hand lifted the glass and lit the lamp on a low table. *It's Mr. Trouble, all right!*

The man had his own secret hideaway. High shelves, shovels, and rakes hid him from the rest of the store. As Libby wondered what to do, she heard more footsteps.

Soon the pawnbroker entered the small area. He carried a violin case. Carefully he set it on the table with the lamp.

Libby felt sure the case was the one she had taken from the pawnbroker's closet. Inside was the violin made from wood more beautiful than anything Libby had ever seen. With all her heart, she believed that violin belonged to Franz Kadosa.

Then the pawnbroker spoke. "Where is he?"

Where is who? Libby wondered and hoped the shopkeeper would return.

"He'll be here in a minute," Mr. Trouble answered.

"Always wants us to do his dirty work," the pawnbroker complained.

A third man is coming? Libby felt weak with dread.

Five minutes. Ten minutes passed. But when the man appeared, Libby was relieved. From her hiding place in the back room, she saw his face. *Annika's friend Mr. White.* In spite of her dislike for him, Libby felt sure Mr. White would help her.

As Libby started to step out, she noticed the man's black coat and the line of his black hat. Libby moved back. *Why does it seem familiar?*

With a jolt Libby knew. The man at the fiddler's concert. The man standing along one side of the *Christina*'s cabin, wearing a long black coat and a black hat. *Shadowman!*

It would have taken only one minute to leave his hat and coat in his stateroom, then walk over to meet Annika!

Now Mr. White walked to the table and the violin case.

"Brought it here like you said," the pawnbroker told him. "I'm expecting an extra cut for doing it. No one saw you carry it through the streets, if that's what you were worried about."

As though barely hearing the pawnbroker, Mr. White nodded. "I'll wrap it in furs when I leave this miserable climate."

Leaning down, Mr. White moved the violin case closer to the lamp. As he opened the cover, the light reflected up on the left side of his face.

Libby gasped. *A red mark just below his jawline!*

She edged back from the doorway. As clearly as if it were yesterday, she remembered the August day the violin was stolen.

The hurried footsteps through a cargo area the thief had probably explored in case he ever needed it. The sound of a door opening and closing. The empty deck on the side away from the gangplank.

The thief had hurried along that deck. He had turned the corner to reach Mr. Oliver White's trunk. A trunk large enough to slip a violin case inside! *All he had to do was catch his breath and stand still!*

Libby's thoughts race on. *So Mr. White hid the violin in the pawnshop. If someone found it here, Mr. White wouldn't be blamed for the theft. No wonder he decided not to sell the violin. He's waiting to use it himself!*

Remembering Annika's words to Pa was the most upsetting of all. *"We have a lot in common,"* she had said about Mr. White. *"We both like music."* What if Annika had let herself be swept away by his money and good looks? Instead, she wanted to marry a man of God!

As Libby thought only of getting away, the pawnbroker spoke. "Where's the girl?"

"In the back room," Mr. Trouble answered.

"Good. Then she's trapped."

Trapped! A cold chill went down Libby's spine. Filled with terror, she wondered if she could move. Then she stretched out her hands and felt her way through an open space in the darkness. *There has to be a back door! But please, God, tell someone I need help!*

Step by slow step, Libby edged her way past shapes that would clatter with one wrong touch. *Don't make a sound.*

A moment later Libby stumbled across something. As she reached out to catch herself, she felt the fur of an animal. A scream rose in her throat.

Libby clapped her hand over her mouth. Standing there in the dark, she started to shake. Then she began to pray. *Oh, God, forgive me. Forgive me for not taking Samson along.*

Waiting, Libby listened for a sound from the front room. Again she prayed. *Please, Lord, lead me out of the dark. Help me be strong in you.*

In that moment she remembered Pa taking her hand. Holding her hand in his, he had given her Ma's cross. Pa's hand felt big compared to her own. *It's that way with God.*

Standing there in the dark, caught between three men and the fur of some unknown animal, Libby told herself again, *It's that way with God.*

As Libby's head cleared, she realized that the animal hadn't moved. Again she reached out. This time when she touched the fur, she felt her way across it. Even in the dark she knew what it was. One of the tightly packed bundles of fur stolen from the warehouse!

Hands out, Libby started walking again. When she bumped against the back wall, she felt her way until she found a door, then the knob.

The door swung open to a third room. To Libby's relief it had two windows and a door. Once again she could see!

No longer could Libby hear the men's voices. Eager now, she moved quickly to the outside door. A strong latch held in place by a big padlock!

Seeing it, Libby felt sick. *"She's trapped,"* the pawnbroker had said. For a moment Libby stared at the door she could not open. When she tested the windows, she found they were nailed shut. Worse still, there were bars on the outside.

Libby groaned. Filled with despair, she sank to the floor.

22

Eagles' Wings

Libby had sat there a full minute before she realized it was ground she sat upon, not a floor. *So this is a shed,* she thought. *An added-on shed, not part of the rest of the building.*

The thought gave her hope again. On her hands and knees she crawled around the outside wall, looking for any possible way out. When she found it, she hardly believed it herself.

At the exact place where the wall met the dirt floor, she saw light, then a hole. *A hole made by an animal,* Libby thought and backed away.

Almost at once she returned to it, knowing it was her only hope. *Can I manage to dig my way out?*

Libby looked around. In the light of the window, she found a strong stick and started making the hole larger.

She had barely begun when she heard sounds from the front of the store. A yapping dog. Angry voices. A dog barking again. Wellington!

Libby could imagine him now. Wellington darting away from the men who would catch him. Wellington circling around, coming close, streaking off. The small dog barking at his big enemies. How had he gotten into the store?

Then Libby remembered Wellington sniffing his way after a

rabbit. Following that rabbit wherever the trail went. *That dog will find me! He'll lead the men right to me before I get out!*

Libby chopped frantically at the dirt. The noise was coming closer now. Wellington's spindly legs were crossing the floor of the middle room.

In the next instant he reached her. At the hole in the outside wall, he began digging. Dirt flew out behind his paws. The hole grew bigger and bigger.

As the terrier slipped through, Libby glanced around. The flickering light of a lantern threw shadows on a wall of the room behind her.

Then she heard voices. Men's voices. Angry voices coming closer and closer.

Desperate now, Libby dropped onto her stomach. When she couldn't make her way through, she twisted onto her back. Digging in with her heels, she wiggled and turned. Finally she squeezed through the hole.

Outside, Libby scrambled up, then caught Wellington. With all her strength she held him in her arms. With her hand around his muzzle, she ordered, "Shush!" Then she crept along the back of the building until she came to a side street.

Without making a sound, Libby hurried to the front side of the building. Near the entrance, she saw fresh footprints in the snow. The smaller ones belonged to Peter. The larger ones were Caleb's.

Hardly daring to breathe, Libby crept close to the door. To her surprise Wellington did not bark, but Libby knew it wouldn't last.

Soon she heard voices from inside. One man talked, and Caleb answered.

Caleb! Someone caught him? Libby felt sick. In four and a half years with the Underground Railroad, he had always escaped from slave catchers. *How did he get caught now?*

Startled, Libby drew back, even more frightened than when she was trapped.

Caleb got caught because of me. He was afraid for me.

Her hand still around Wellington's muzzle, Libby crept away. The dog wiggled and squirmed, clearly upset. It took all Libby's strength to hang on.

It took her a moment to remember where the police station was. Then Libby walked as fast as she could. Close to the station, she let Wellington down. "Go find Peter!" The dog streaked away.

In two minutes Libby had explained to the police. All of them had seen her drawing of Mr. Trouble. As they hurried off, she followed close behind.

Moving without sound, the policemen entered the store. A short time later they led the three men away.

"The shopkeeper?" Libby asked Caleb when it was all over. "Did he know he was hiding stolen property?"

Caleb shook his head. "He thought the furs belonged to Mr. White. I heard Mr. White offer to close up for the day. He told the shopkeeper he could go home."

That made Libby curious. "The crooks had another store— the pawnshop. Why did they meet in this one?"

"For some reason they needed to use the building. The way it sounded, they had planned their biggest theft yet."

In the late afternoon light, Libby saw relief in Caleb's eyes. Yet as the three of them walked to Annika's, it was Peter, not Caleb, who told Libby what happened.

"When you didn't come to Annika's, we went looking for you. Caleb said you didn't want him along. He figured that meant you would buy art supplies, so he knew where to look. We saw your sign of the fish and went inside. Caleb heard one of the men talking about how you snooped around the pawnshop."

"And your dog?" Libby asked.

"When the men caught us, I used my secret signal to send Wellington after you. He's a hero, isn't he?"

Libby smiled. "Yes, Wellington is a hero," she signed. Motioning with her hands, she dug with all her might to show how the terrier had dug out the hole. "He's not a mutt!"

Pointing to Peter, Libby signed again. "You're a hero too. You taught Wellington to obey you!"

Peter beamed with pride. "I told you he was a good dog."

Libby smiled, but Caleb still did not speak. Libby wondered about it.

Then Peter said, "In two days it's Thanksgiving! We can give the fiddler his violin then!"

The next morning Caleb and Libby walked into St. Paul to meet Jordan. As the three of them started back to the *Christina*, Libby glanced ahead. In a yard close to where they would pass was a tall, strong-looking boy with a snowball in his hand. Again and again he smoothed the ball, rubbing and packing it tight. Libby felt sure it was no longer snow but a chunk of ice as hard as a rock.

In a low voice, Caleb spoke. "He's looking for trouble."

"I see him," Jordan said.

A moment later the boy disappeared. As Libby, Caleb, and Jordan drew close, they watched the yard, the house, and a large oak with a thick trunk.

Suddenly a snowball whizzed out toward Jordan's head. Jordan saw it coming and ducked.

Libby gasped. Caleb and Jordan headed for the tree.

Just then the boy stepped out. In his hand he held another ice ball. On the ground beside him lay a mound of ammunition waiting to be used. But Jordan walked straight up to the boy.

Two feet away Jordan stopped. "Why did you do that?"

The boy sneered. "Because of who you are."

His fists clenched, Jordan took another step toward the boy. Glaring down at him, Jordan met the boy's gaze. "There's two of us bigger than you."

"I'm not scared. I'll take on both of you. And I'll win."

"No," Jordan said. "You won't win."

He straightened, standing tall. Then he uncurled his fingers and walked away.

He walked with his eyes on the boy so he wouldn't be hit by another ice ball.

Two blocks later, Jordan finally spoke. "I did it!" he exclaimed as if he were the most surprised person alive. "I walked away! I didn't have to prove myself to him."

The next day Micah Parker brought his family by sleigh from

St. Anthony. As Serena and the others came on board, Libby knew that all of them truly had become one big family.

A few minutes later, Franz walked up the gangplank. When he took off his coat, he still wore the tattered shirt, but now Libby felt sure she knew what it meant. Franz wore ragged clothing to disguise who he was.

Today his step was even lighter than when he danced for the deckers. As everyone sat down in the *Christina's* winter room, Franz looked around the circle. "Yesterday Caleb told me that you have a big surprise for me. First, I want to tell you my story.

"Before I came here today, I went to the jail. Two of the men would not talk to me. But it was Oliver White I wanted to meet. At the concert, the man in the shadows seemed familiar. I knew if he was someone from my days in Vienna, he could betray me."

"Betray you?" All along, Libby had felt sure there was someone the fiddler could not trust.

"My real name is not Kadosa. In my homeland of Hungary I am part of a noble family. They could not understand why I wanted to study the violin. But my music is here." Franz laid his hand on his heart.

"In the last revolution, my family lost our cause and fell out of favor with the rulers. Some of my loved ones died. Others fled to America."

"The family near Nicollet," Libby said.

Franz nodded. "At first I thought I could stay in Hungary. Then I learned that I couldn't. When I needed to escape, my wife and children went into hiding. From one hiding place to the next, they worked their way to the border. Now they hide in a neighboring country, waiting for word from me. That is why I did not tell my secrets. I need to protect them."

"And you needed to learn if you could trust us," Caleb said.

"You knew it was a risk to play for first-class passengers, didn't you?" Pa asked.

"I wondered if some of them had traveled in Europe and could recognize me."

"Is that why you use German words?" Libby asked.

"If I spoke Hungarian, a person who understood the language would know where I am from."

Libby was still curious. "How would Oliver White know you?"

"At the jail, I looked into his eyes and recognized him. We were students in Vienna when there were tryouts for a well-known orchestra. We competed against each other. He is a very good violinist, but I won the place."

"He was jealous?" Caleb asked. "He wanted to get even?"

Franz nodded. "At first. But there was more. He knew my violin is gut value. He knew the money it might bring. Because he couldn't get the amount he wanted, he decided to keep the violin. He thought that if he had such a fine instrument, he would become the violinist he always wanted to be."

"He's like a little boy, isn't he?" Annika said. "He doesn't understand that for someone to play music in a way that touches people, he must feel the music by how he lives."

"My land and wealth are gone," Franz answered. "But if I have my fiddle, I can earn a living. That's why I watched how you treated Jordan."

In that moment Libby had the answer to another puzzle. "You watched during school? You were the one looking through the window?"

As the fiddler nodded, he looked young again. "I knew that if you gave to Jordan the freedom he needs, you will give my family the freedom we need."

"But no matter where you live, there will be someone who doesn't want to do that," Caleb said. "Someone who tries to take freedom from others."

The fiddler smiled. "But as long as there are people who rob us of freedom, there need to be others like you and Libby, Jordan, and Peter." Franz looked around the room. "People like all of you who work to keep freedom for others."

It was Peter who gave Franz his violin. As though unable to believe he truly held it again, the fiddler ran his fingers across the wood. Then he began to tune his treasured violin.

When Franz looked up, Libby saw the tears in his eyes. When he spoke, she heard the tears in his voice. "I will tell my family I have found a new home. And now I will play for you a song I learned from a special friend."

The sweet, mellow tones of his violin filled the room. As he played, Libby heard the words in her mind.

Deep River, my home is over Jordan;
Deep River; Lord, I want to cross over into camp ground.

Annika reached out her hand. While Pa held it in his, the music soared around them. In that moment Libby understood what Jordan had known all along.

Live freedom? To be strong enough to let myself be free? That's what it is! To believe, truly believe, that no matter what happens to me, God can work in everything to bring something good.

As the *Christina*'s family gathered around one large table, Gran and Annika, Hattie Parker, Serena, and Libby brought out the food they had prepared. But Libby knew it wasn't the food that mattered.

Pa looked from one person to the next. "Before we eat, let's give thanks for all that God has done for us."

It started with Pa's teasing. "I'm thankful that Annika knew she was supposed to be in St. Paul this winter."

But soon it turned serious. "I'm thankful that you adopted me," Peter told Libby and Pa.

Jordan's mother looked around the table at her family. "I still need to pinch myself—to say, 'Hattie, you and your family are free.' I thank the good Lord that we are together."

Micah grinned. "And I'm thankful that I have a job to support you." In spite of the panic, a man at one of the flour mills had hired Micah to take care of his horses.

When Jordan explained how he walked away from the bully, he said, "I'm thankful that God helped me live freedom."

Then Annika spoke. "I'm glad I can be part of your never-give-up family." Her gaze rested on each of them, but under the tablecloth she again held Pa's hand.

"I'm thankful for something I've learned," Libby said. "Even when things are awful and nothing makes sense, God can bring something good."

The fiddler spoke last of all. "When I needed to flee my country, I promised my wife I would find a place for our family. I traveled in rags because I wanted a true feeling for America. I wanted to know how people would treat a poor man—a man who is not famous."

Franz smiled. "That is my biggest secret—that I told my family I would find a place where people are kind. Today I am thankful I can keep my promise to them."

Later, when everyone had eaten and the dishes were washed and put away, Libby went outside. On the hurricane deck she found Caleb. He stood looking beyond the island, upriver to the bluffs and the city of St. Paul.

At first neither of them spoke, but then Libby was curious. "Caleb, when we talked about being thankful, you didn't say anything."

"I couldn't in front of everyone else."

As Caleb looked at her, Libby saw the pain in his eyes. "When I knew you were trapped in that store with the three crooks—" Caleb shook his head. "It was even worse than Peter with the rattlesnake."

Then Caleb, who had never betrayed a fugitive by giving away his thoughts, brushed a hand across his eyes. "I'm thankful that you're my friend, Libby. I'm thankful to God that you are home and you are safe."

In the spring of the year, Pa began building again. He took Libby's room and the one behind it and enlarged his own cabin for a family place. He gave Libby the space just behind that and Peter the room next to hers so they would always be close to the rest of the family.

Then when the time was right, Pa asked Annika to marry him.

Because Libby was trying very hard to grow up, she did *not* listen in and never heard what Pa said. Libby only knew how he and Annika looked. Their eyes and faces seemed filled with light. They could not stop smiling, and they talked often about the goodness of God.

When the ice went out of Lake Pepin, Pa said it was time to

drop south again. Caleb's grandmother knew what that meant, and she began making a huge wedding cake and every kind of food fit for a feast.

The morning that Annika came on board was bright and clear and the sky so blue that it took Libby's breath away. As the *Christina* steamed down the river, Libby searched out Annika. There was something that weighed on Libby's mind. She needed to set it straight.

She found Annika in the place that had always been one of Libby's favorites—high on the *Christina* at the front of the hurricane deck. Today Annika had woven a strand of pearls through her black hair. In every way she looked a bride.

"Annika?" Libby asked, and the young woman turned. But when Libby tried to speak, her throat felt tight and uncomfortable.

"What is it, Libby?" Annika asked.

"Remember how you said that a mother can be a friend? But that a mother also needs to tell me what I'm doing wrong so I learn to change it?"

Annika nodded.

"You were right, Annika. When you said to keep Samson with me, I should have listened to you."

"Yes," Annika agreed.

"I could have been badly hurt."

"Yes," Annika said again.

"I can't promise that I'll always listen." Again Libby stumbled over her words. "That I'll ever be perfect."

"No, you can't." Annika smiled. "I can't either."

At last Libby relaxed. "There's something I want you to know. I want to be friends. But I also want you to be my mother."

Tears welled up in Annika's eyes and ran down her cheeks. "Thank you, Libby. You honor me with your gift."

At Red Wing the *Christina* stopped long enough to pick up a friend of Pa's—a pastor he had known for some time. Then through Lake Pepin they went and below that to a quiet place in the backwaters.

There the crew tied up along the shore. With the trees on a nearby island wearing their spring-green best, Pa and Annika were married.

As best man, Caleb stood straight and tall next to Pa. Libby was maid of honor for Annika, and Peter held the rings.

"Do you take this man to be your lawfully wedded husband?" the pastor asked Annika.

With her strong yet gentle voice she spoke her vows: "For better, for worse, for richer, for poorer, in sickness and in health, to love and to cherish, till death us do part."

When Pa spoke his vows, Libby didn't hear them, for just then she remembered Annika's words. *She said she wouldn't marry till she found a man of God who loved and cherished her the way she wanted to cherish him.*

As it all became real, Libby's heart leaped. *Annika found him! And Pa found her!*

Then, as her father and her new mother exchanged rings, Libby's thoughts ran on. *I wonder if I'll have the courage of Annika—to wait until I find a man who truly loves God and also loves me?*

Looking beyond Annika to Pa, Libby saw Caleb. *I think I already know who I want to marry when I grow up. But what if he meets someone else and decides he loves that girl instead?*

As though a shadow passed over the sun, the thought frightened Libby. *What's ahead for Caleb and me? What good things? What hard things? What will we have to face?*

Once again the pastor's voice broke into Libby's thoughts. As Annika and Pa clasped their hands together, the pastor placed his hand on top of theirs. "Nathaniel and Annika, I now pronounce you man and wife. The Lord bless you and keep you."

In that moment Libby heard the flutter of wings as two eagles rose from a stream in the backwaters. Against the bright blue of the sky, they soared away together.

Libby watched the eagles until they disappeared. When she looked back to the *Christina*, she found Caleb watching her. *God wants us to soar*, Libby thought as her smile met his. *In whatever comes to us, God wants us to soar!*

THE MANUAL
Alphabet

Courtesy of the Illinois
School for the Deaf, Jacksonville.

Acknowledgments

While writing this series, I've received many heartwarming letters from you, my very special readers. Often you've said that these novels have changed your life.

Usually you begin by telling how much you like to read about the excitement and suspense of the Underground Railroad. You talk about Jordan's courage in working for the freedom of his family. You mention Libby, Caleb, Pa, Gran, Peter, or the free blacks and whites who risked their freedom, reputation, and property for what they believed.

Then you say, "There's something I've wondered. If I had lived in 1857, would I have been one of those who helped runaway slaves reach freedom?"

Your question is an important one because you are really asking, "Would I know what I believe about the important things going on around me?" Then, "Would I have the courage to act upon what I believe?"

You might find the answer by asking still another question: "How do I treat the people who are around me right now? People of other races and ethnic groups; my family; the kid who's being picked on by bullies; the boy or girl who dresses in a way that's different from everyone else; or the person who is really hungry?"

Jordan wanted a home where his family could live safe and free. The fiddler wanted a place where people would be kind to his family. Isn't that the same love and kindness that each of us needs to receive? And every one of us needs to give?

If you know the answer to these questions, you have learned something that will help you the rest of your life.

For many years a number of people have offered special kindness to me. Big thanks to all of you who have faithfully encouraged and supported my writing. Your caring hearts have helped me continue.

Captain Retired Dennis Trone, builder of the *Twilight* and the *Julia Belle Swain* and for twenty-four years captain of the *Julia Belle Swain*, shared his piloting experience, imagination, and love of steamboats and the river. Thanks, Captain, for the exciting fog and ice scenes, the rattlesnake's appearance, and your strong sense of story. Captain Trone is also the former owner of the Marine Hospital in Galena, Illinois.

My appreciation to the state of Illinois and the people responsible for the terrific camping at the Mississippi Palisades State Park. Along with Libby, Caleb, and Peter, we've enjoyed your incredible view.

Freelance editor and violinist Helen Motter answered my many questions about playing the violin, helped me develop my character Franz, and read portions of the manuscript. Robert Miller, former curator at the *George M. Verity*, the Keokuk River Museum and National Historic Landmark at Keokuk, Iowa, also answered questions for this and nearly every RIVERBOAT novel.

Kathleen Cook, second grade teacher at the Illinois School for the Deaf at Jacksonville, helped me with sign language and my character Peter. Thanks for your time in reading the manuscript, Kathy, and your ideas about a terrier as wonderful as Wellington. Kevin Healy, a student at the same school, inspired me by teaching his dog to obey sign language. Joan Forney, superintendent, gave permission to use the finger alphabet chart in this book.

If you haven't visited St. Paul, you'll be glad to know that the streets have not remained in their 1857 condition. The present streets and freeways offer lovely approaches to the downtown area and the Minnesota State Capitol.

My gratitude to Kate Roberts, exhibit curator, and the Minnesota State Historical Society for your research facility and journal, *Minnesota History.*

Thanks to the Ramsey County Historical Society for your journal, *Ramsey County History*, and the help of Julie Reimnitz, administrative manager and researcher, and Mollie Spillman, curator archivist. I am especially indebted to Virginia Brainard Kunz, the Society's former director, for her books, *St. Paul: The First 150 Years*; *The Mississippi and St. Paul*; and *St. Paul: Saga of an American City.*

Virginia also answered many questions, as did Rhoda R. Gilman. Thanks, Rhoda, for your book *The Story of Minnesota's Past* and your coauthoring of *The Red River Trails.* Thanks to June Drenning Holmquist, editor of *They Chose Minnesota*, and authors David Vassar Taylor, Paul Kirchner, and Anne R. Kaplan.

Two persons gave me the thought I needed at just the right time: Dr. Charles L. Blockson, author of *The Underground Railroad*, and Miles McPherson, author of *The Power of Believing in Your Child.* I am also grateful for the insights of Sven Sjostedt, columnist and freelance writer; Lisa Krahn, site manager, Sibley Historic Site; John Anfinson, district historian, Army Corps of Engineers, St. Paul; Greg Brick, geologist; Catherine Mix, editorial assistant, *The Minnesota Volunteer*; and the *St. Paul Pioneer Press* for their early *Pioneer and Democrat* newspapers. Roger Mackey, Louie Morelli, and Bette Johnson helped me with the Swede Hollow area.

As always, thanks to the entire Bethany team for taking my books through the publishing process, then bringing them to my readers. Special gratitude to Jeanne Mikkelson, publicity director, and my in-house editors, Rochelle Glöege and Natasha Sperling, for persevering with me and caring about me as a person.

This novel marks the twentieth book that my out-of-house editor, Ron Klug, has edited for me. Thanks, Ron, for the amazing, life-giving way you have helped shape my work. You've earned a very big award, especially in the hearts of my readers.

Finally, I'm grateful to my husband, Roy, to each of our children, their spouses, and our grandchildren. You've brought richness, truth, and a sense of humor to our life together. By being the terrific persons you are, you have profoundly influenced my thinking and writing. Thanks to each one of you!